CW00957506

SPLITHEAD

Splithead

JULYA RABINOWICH

Translated from the German by Tess Lewis

Portobello
BOOKS

Published by Portobello Books 2011

Portobello Books
12 Addison Avenue
London W11 4QR

Originally published as *Spaltkopf* by Exil Verlag, Vienna, in 2009.

The publication of this work was supported by a grant from
the Austrian Federal Ministry for Education, Arts and Culture.

A CIP catalogue record is available from the British Library

9 8 7 6 5 4 3 2 1

ISBN 978 1 84627 282 0

www.portobellobooks.com

Text designed and typeset by Lindsay Nash

Printed in the UK by J F Print Ltd., Sparkford, Somerset.

Bitten Off, Not Torn

Hop, skip, cut

BILE-GREEN WHEREVER YOU LOOK – WATER, SKY, COASTLINE, all the same shade – like me, feeling downright cool. I am taking a trip. I'm on board a ferry that is just leaving Ireland for Scotland. I'm pregnant and I'm convinced I look gutsy.

I jump again. My game is hopscotch from one land to another. It would be unwise to miss one; you'd get eliminated. The other players are still out. They're in Russia, waiting to leave for Israel. At this point, some of them still have no idea how lucky they are; others don't know that one day they will turn their backs on this destination, too. Go on home, shoo, shoo, back in your basket.

It's boring when you're out. You watch the player whose turn it is and comment on his moves. This distracts him and speeds up the turns. My father's out and it's my turn.

So, I'm travelling. I never did arrive, not on my first trip, not after my second. The journey is not ending and the holiday is long. I'll refuse to pay the travel expenses.

The coastal strip looks like it's been bitten off; you can clearly see its layers of flesh. I feel like I've been bitten off as well, because the land I came from doesn't cling to me and I don't cling to it. No strings tie me to it any more.

This trip will take me in succession through Scotland, Holland, Vienna and through the birth of my daughter. Between Glasgow and Amsterdam, I feel my child take her first steps in my belly. It throws me into a panic. Even my daughter has already set off on a journey. So we're both in transit.

LESSON 1

Whoever is crazy now will be for a long time.
They'll read, roam and write long letters.

I'm sitting with my parents, my grandmother Ada and my doll in the plane. All the players are frozen (in standby mode). The chocolate sweet, a Mozart ball, melts in my hand, but its colourful wrapper seems too valuable to tear off. I've never seen anything like it before.

I'm convinced, because of what my parents told me, that we're heading to Lithuania for a holiday. Shortly before landing, there's a difference of opinion. Another child insists we're flying to Vienna and refuses to change her mind. I'm meant to be the one who's mistaken.

The toilet is a palace and the chewing-gum dispensers promise a beautiful new world. The four of us live in one room in a hotel that seems to be a brothel. So I'm put in solitary confinement and am not allowed outside.

My father and I both suffer nervous breakdowns when he tries

4

to exorcise three years of Communist socialization in one evening and I simply cannot comprehend that Lenin, friend of all children, whose pin is still emblazoned on my dress (lost in the excitement of the trip), is suddenly an arsehole.

What my father can't do one glimpse of a Barbie doll does. In five minutes I'm converted to the West. I'll remain so for a long time. Years later, I can barely remember not being born here. I'm prepared to speak German better than my classmates. I'm prepared to go voluntarily to catechism classes, while the Turkish children get to go home early. I'm prepared to imitate prayers, whose words at first aren't clear to me. Later, it will be other dogmas. To be part of a group – as long as it isn't too big – I'm ready to sell my soul to the devil, even if they're only interested in LSD. I'm willing to spend twice my salary on eccentric clothing, even if it means I'll suffer agonizing money problems at work afterwards.

The objectionable whiff from a little immigrant girl can't simply be washed away with Chanel. A loss must be recovered right away – instantly. The emptiness can't be left yawning for a single moment.

I go shopping when my father dies.

I go shopping when I break up with my first boyfriend.

LESSON 2

Travellers should not be detained.

My father goes on a final journey and leaves behind for me, as a small souvenir, a debilitating fear of trips of every kind. For a time, I turn into a display case of neuroses: claustrophobia and agoraphobia, fear of flying, fear of tunnels, trains, relationships and death. Robbed of my range of movement, I begin spiralling round myself.

I'm often sick.

I write.

I get caught up in endlessly complicated love affairs.

They are as convoluted as the paths I'm not able to follow.

The world is round.

Once you let loose, you can't stop any more. Soon you're drawn over the edge, then still further. You advance like a skipjack. There's hardly an inclination that can flatten you. Longing wells up for the good old days when turtles and elephants held up the disc of the world! It would have been so easy to sneak up to the edge, peer over the side and be done with it.

But our kind sits on the carousel, even though we're close to vomiting.

I'm on my way back to myself through drugs, analysis and bouts of work.

I'm a bulimic perpetual-motion machine spasmodically plagued by the desire to incorporate and the inability to retain anything.

In short, I've adapted.

The world is round.

LESSON 4

Fast-forward.

I'm standing on a mountain spur, looking into the depths: the Rhône meanders at my feet. France is to my left; to my right, the abyss.

The wind is warm. Early signs of spring are everywhere.

The water in my river is sluggish. Yellow and bilious, it rolls on.

Faced with a choice between two stools, I take the bed of nails.

I am tired.

I'm not home.

I have arrived.

The Dogs of Ostia

1

WHEN MY MOTHER WAS PREGNANT WITH ME, SHE OFTEN
sat at her vanity table, gazing into the mirror for a long time and
imagining what her child would look like. Before her lay a book.
'*Russian Fairy Tales*' was stamped on its worn cloth cover in gold
lettering. Her hand, small and elegant, rested on an open page
below the title 'Mistress of the Copper Mountain'. There are many
stories about her, and all of them open with a majestic flourish of
a letter, Cyrillic. On the facing page is an illustration protected
with crinkling tissue paper. Behind the dull veil, its colours can
only be imagined. The picture shows a woman with a long, black
plait leaning against a wall of malachite. Her dress, her eyes –
which appear watchful and stern – and the malachite necklace
round her pale throat are all the same colour. She sinks into a sea
of green, dissolves into it. My mother looks at her and wishes for
a girl with skin as white as snow and lips as red as blood.

The fire blazes in the fireplace lined with crumbling marble slabs.
Displayed on the broad stone mantel are Father's treasures, found

at the junk shop or dug out of the rubbish. Heavy cast-iron candle-sticks, small statuettes, copper mugs, lovingly arranged and each piece perfectly capable of breaking my curious nose if I happen to bump it off the mantel. The warped image of my eyes, reflected in the brass border of the hearth, distracts me – strange spots that follow my movements, until I slip and lose my footing. One foot falls into the darkness behind the grate. I climb my way back up and edge, hand over hand, along the front of the fireplace, the treasures back in my sights, within reach, my slippers now covered in ash.

On my left rises my father Lev's tall, carved chair. Like every tribal founding father, he has his throne. On one of his excursions to the dump, he found it under countless layers of dirt, freed it and polished it to a new shine. The dark brown lions' heads on the back bare their teeth at me in warning.

Father sits at the centre of the big table, round which our rela-tives have gathered. They're immersed in their farewell party, waving crystal glasses, sandwiches and the cheese biscuits my mother courageously baked in the kitchen of our communal apart-ment once she managed to fend off an angry storm of neighbours from one of the two ovens.

I am a princess. Kings and queens are on my side; nothing can happen to me. I circle the heavy table in wobbly pirouettes.

So much has been laid out on the table that the guests have no room for their elbows or hands. There is 'herring-in-a-fur-coat', with its glowing white mantle of sour cream shading into light pink towards the centre, where the purple slices of beetroot cover a bed of potatoes layered with salted fish. It's a winter landscape, decorated with white onion rings and, here and there, sprigs of green parsley. The untouched dish looks as soft and rounded as a feather pillow. Only because it's so beautiful do I take an enormous serving, which I leave untouched after one bite. There is a small bowl of red caviar, and next to it one of black. There are bowls of salad, biscuits, tarts, carafes of red and white wine, frosted bottles of vodka. In the corner, on a small side table, stands a rusty, swelling electric samovar and, next to it, the watery marmalade with chunks of fruit that traditionally accompanies the tea.

Outside, it's bitterly cold; darkness sets in around three o'clock in the afternoon. My athletic grandmother Ada, my beautiful mother Laura's mother, curses as she drags me on a sledge through the streets of St Petersburg, barely recognizable in the driving snow and massive drifts covering the roofs and pavements. Over our winter shoes, we wear additional boots of black boiled wool, and over that rubber slippers, the northern version of rubber boots, called *valenki*.

Just like accumulated primary matter before the Big Bang, the family is now concentrated round this enormous table full of loot; some will fly to America, others will disperse to Israel, some to South Africa and Japan, and we will build our galaxy round the constantly revolving sun of Austria, until such time as the heat on our heavenly bodies lessens and conditions more conducive to life are established on our surfaces.

All branches of the family are here. A rough classification of the guests gives you mathematicians, painters and former painters, architects and former architects and their dependants in a ratio of approximately fifty-fifty. Edward, my mother's brother, his wife, Olga, with their two children, Adrian and Anastasia, a thin boy with glasses and the graceful, eight-year-old prima ballerina.

I have a bone to pick with Uncle Edward. Too often I can feel his disapproving gaze on me and my plump, unfit body, while his daughter, with her long, dark plait, floats through the room in svelte loveliness. My hair is cut in a detested pageboy, the family's curse. My grandmother Ada's is light red, my mother's raven black. They both wear thick, dark eyeliner. Ada also wears lipstick. They both look elegant, an offence in socialist Russia.

Scowling, I try to tame the thin, feathering hair on the nape of my neck with a band. We don't have any elastics for my hair, just yard-long strips of semi-transparent nylon. The trick is to wind it up into an especially poufy bouquet. Adrian is a balm to my imperfection. His ears stick out and don't look particularly fortunate next to his sister's glowing eyes. I give him a sympathetic look. He sticks his long, veined tongue out at me. It matches his nose. Later, he will build slender glass towers in New York.

The doorbell of our communal apartment rings. My mother goes to open the door. The neighbour, Aunt Musja, stumbles into the hallway in her Crimplene bathrobe and rants at her. She wants to sleep, not listen to our carousing. Her tiny room is right next to our rooms and two guests have already unexpectedly forced their way into her place, without even knocking, because they confused the doors. The walls are paper-thin. The hallways are long and rambling.

My father's sister, Ljuba, arrives in a cloud of peculiar, spicy-sweet perfume, with her twin daughters, Ninotschka and Lenotschka. The room suddenly seems overcrowded. Each of them tips the scales at 200 pounds. They file ceremoniously into the room, each bearing an overloaded tray in her soft arms. All three smile seductively and lift the broad cloth napkins. A murmur spreads through the room. I am pleased. On the one hand, there are now delicious pastries; on the other, I'm no longer the fattest child in the room.

Aunt Ljuba balances on Mother's elegant Biedermeier chair. Her groans sink in the laughter and shouting. She's called Lubov, which means 'love' in Russian, Ljuba for short. There is enough to go around. She arranges her colourful silk shawl over her round shoulders and kisses Lev, her brother. Her pretty face fades into a double chin. Ninotschka and Lenotschka hang on her like two cherubs – an overflowing feminine Laocoön. I almost nestled in with them. The ballerina's disgusted look stopped me just in time. I step back and look at them just as contemptuously. We're separated by almost eighty pounds.

My father's youngest brother, Nathanael, and his wife, Vera, are sitting across from him. They look like failed replicas of my parents. Since Nathanael copies everything my father does, he has let his beard grow. He's an architect, too, like Lev. As in the story of the tortoise and the hare, Nathanael is damned to limp for ever behind his brother. No matter what he does, Lev is always there first. He seems even to have chosen his partner, Vera, by my mother's example. The two women sit there now in their similar purple outfits and smile painfully at each other from beneath their dark fringes. Nathanael drapes his arm possessively around Vera's narrow shoulders, while Laura's delicate shoulder snuggles up against my father's rough sweater.

At that moment, Salomon, Lev's middle brother, waves his vodka glass so emphatically that half its contents spill onto the tablecloth and the dress of his unlikely companion, Lida. She looks over her glasses at him weakly. He is macho. He has a big nose and surprisingly pale skin. He is the only blonde in the whole group. His eyes, as turquoise blue as my father's, squint slightly down his nose. For the huge bump on it, he can thank Lev, who thirty-five years ago had flailed at him with a pair of shears in childish boisterousness. Maybe that's why he didn't want to be a painter or an architect. He's a plumber.

Above the fireplace hangs a hackneyed black-and-white photograph in an enamel frame. It shows a bald man in an army uniform with a good-natured, dull-witted smile and a drinker's nose. That is Uncle Vanya, a war veteran, our pseudo-grandfather, whom our dead great-grandmother Rivka picked up during the war. He raised my uncle Edward, my mother and me. A disabled war orphan, Rivka's apparently never consummated love. A piece of shrapnel, visible even in this grainy shot, is lodged in his skull near his temple, half covered with skin. He spent his last forty years in disability retirement and, aside from drunken binges on every quarterly payday with our building's Armenian alcoholic, he devoted most of his time to raising the family child of the moment. He has been dead for a year, but to protect me, no-one has told me yet. I am still outraged by his long absence, which for me means acute chocolate deprivation.

We are celebrating. They laugh because they don't want to cry. They know something I don't. I don't know that they know what I don't. That said, I know something they don't. Furious that they're paying so little attention to me, I have been into the kitchen and have spat into the large porcelain bowl of Russian salad that I don't like anyway, and now I watch, spellbound, to see who will get the moistened part. The record player serves up jazz and Mozart. Outside, the snow blusters. Inside, the children storm, even though they'd been herded into my grandmother's room and put to bed.

Ljuba, cloaked in her furs, has long since boarded the last yellow trolley bus for home with the thickly hooded twins. We had better go to bed, my mother threatens, her voice and finger raised, 'Or Splithead will come.'

Adrian laughs. Anastasia and I exchange nervous looks.

Grandma Ada joins in. Apparently she can already hear him coming up the stairs.

'He's almost here. If you don't disappear under the covers, he will hover over you and eat your thoughts.'

'He'll suck your souls right out of you!' Grandma Ada opens the door invitingly.

I have never gone into the side room so quickly. On my scale of terrifying things, Splithead beats Baba Yaga, who lives in a hut perched on chicken legs. This Russian witch is sometimes helpful and good, which can't be said of Splithead.

My grandmother Ada says he's a spectre – at best, an indifferent spectre.

This hovering one has a special place in Russian mythology. Both Baba Yaga and Splithead can fly. She uses a cauldron, in which she squats and, with a ladle, stirs, so to speak, her own juices to steer her flight. All Splithead needs is human energy.

'He doesn't have a body,' my mother whispered to me last winter over a crackling candle flame on the bedside table as the flickering twisted her features into something different, something strange. As soon as the flame steadied, once her warm breath stopped making it dance, her face regained its familiar expression and no longer frightened me.

'He's invisible.' Her eyes gleamed.

'He's just a huge, floating head that hovers over people. And then . . . he sucks them dry. If they aren't careful.'

I squirm with tension. 'Isn't there anything, anything at all you can do to stop him?' I whisper.

'Of course, Mischka, of course,' my mother says. 'You have to see him. If you can see him, then he has no power over you.'

My unloved cousins are put on a creaky metal folding bed and covered with a blanket of raw felting made from Uncle Vanya's army coat and decorated with braiding. Disgustingly well behaved as usual, they go straight to sleep after the briefest protest.

I lie awake and try hard to catch bits of conversation from the next room. We only have two rooms. My parents and I live in the big one, Ada in the smaller. The high double doors that separate us are ajar and a small ray of light shines in through the crack. As

I listen, I glue my lashes together with spit. Now I'm an eyeless newt that has never seen a ray of sunlight deep in an underground lake and I must find my way using only my hearing. Then, I take inspiration from the crack of the open doors and masturbate lethargically. Just before I finally sink into a wintry dream, I hear my grandmother's thundering voice announce, 'Whoever doesn't eat this cake spits on my soul!' immediately followed by the sound of spoons scraping on plates.

While some sleep and the others dream, so pass the night, the morning and the following day.

They lie to themselves and they lie to the child as well.
It does not affect me.
They keep me alive.
The womb full of blood, the fresh drops of sperm on the skin.
That is the ink with which I, their chronicler, capture their lives.
She wants to forget and not to forgive.
I forget nothing and forgive nothing.
Igor. Not Israil.
The number and the word and the knowledge.

My path takes me past the customs officers. Weighed down with red-gold insignia and medals hung on expanses of green, they awaken festive New Year's sentiments in me. Behind the cordon, level with my nose, and into the long corridor. We are in the middle of our departure to Western Europe. According to the average Russian citizen's level of knowledge at the time, we might as well be on the border of the USSR and the moon. In our luggage, which will go missing several days later, we have packed, along with the emigrants' usual absurdities, several pounds of buckwheat flour, which our rather anti-Semitic Georgian neighbours have offered us as a goodbye present in their patriotic concern that we could starve in Austria. My parents, accompanied by my grandmother Ada, already have their rebirth behind them. They stand in the corridor that leads to the aeroplane.

I step into the corridor. At its near end are gathered the wailing relatives who will remain in the Soviet Union. At the far end shines the light of a new world.

I have no inkling of any of this. I'm possessed by the urge to turn back at this point. Baba Sara, my father's tiny mother, has stayed behind the dividing line. She stands there tensely, fingers clenched round a packet of strong cigarettes, which she holds hidden in the roomy pocket of her rose-covered kaftan. Sara has draped the still-thick plait that reaches down to her hips over her chest. With her other hand, she tries to spread her tears across the lavender circles round her eyes as she smiles, smiles, smiles and, every once in a while, waves at me cheerfully with her wet fingers.

I want to hug her one last time. Baba Sara looks so much like me that, even at the age of seven, I know what I will look like when I'm sixty-five. Past and future approach each other briefly, I as her memory and she as the image of my future. Time wavers. When we touch, we envelop each other like two waves rolling together. A many-voiced howl rises from both sides. If I cross the barrier, the officials threaten to send me from heaven back to earth. Stopped by my family's screams, I brake right before the turnstile. I turn away from Baba Sara and walk slowly towards the exit. I don't look back.

I will no longer look back.

Our plane takes off. My seven-year past shrinks behind me beyond recognition, like my beloved white dress, hand-knit by my mother, which was inadvertently put on a hot wash. If I'm lucky, my dolls will be able to wear both.

The elephant-grey concrete mess that is the Palace of the Pioneers. The house where I was born on Vasilievsky Island, with its bridges over the Neva all raised at night so the large ships can pass, only to have their metal teeth bite into each other again in the early morning hours, primeval dinosaur necks against the continuously pink skies of the white nights. Confusing extended family relations. The national hymn in nursery school: we played 'Lenin Returns Home' and handed out papier-mâché flowers. My dark brown school uniform, whose resemblance to a bourgeois governess's outfit I did not notice until after I'd been in Vienna for a long time. My October Child badge is still stuck on my jumper. The red bouquets for the parades, and the shop shelves swept clean. Our communal apartment with its varied tenants, Schenya, my first love, whose nose I had, not long before, bloodied by pushing him into a tree out of jealousy. The stories I grew up with, which accompanied me night after night into the future: 'The Mistress of Copper Mountain', who can change herself into a lizard and who richly rewards good men with jewels and crushes the bad between the walls of her mountain. She is green-eyed and mysterious. Baba Yaga, who wades through the swamp in her little hut on chicken legs. Sometimes she helps people who seek her out because they have no other choice; sometimes she devours them, depending on her mood. Splithead, who lives off the thoughts and feelings of others, an impassive vampire, watchful, invisible, menacing, but who is still unpleasantly personal, a private monster, custom-made and set upon our family.

My aunt Ljuba told her children that there was a bottle in the cellar with a hellhound in it. Now my cousins won't even go near the cellar door out of fear that the sound of their footsteps could wake the monster. But in their cellar are only a few cases of homemade liquor, hidden under old newspapers. This hellhound – always ready to jump out of his bottle – can be found in almost every communal apartment building. He is cared for and fed.

Friends and foes – all scatter behind the engines that rock me to sleep. I'm convinced by my parents' account of our trip: we're flying to Lithuania on holiday. So the tearful parting in the airport strikes me as rather excessive. There is a girl my age on the plane. I get into a violent argument with her because she dares lie to my face. 'We're not flying to Vienna,' I tell her.

She claims I'm wrong.

The gold-foil wrapper of the chocolate Mozart ball handed out on the plane is too beautiful to destroy. The perfect shape melts in my hand as I admire it. Later, I will stubbornly look for my homeland, like a stupid dog that has been taken several miles away and persistently tries to run back in the wrong direction.

In preparation, my parents keep me in the dark even through the weeks leading up to our departure. As piles of boxes begin to tower over me, there is talk of renovating the apartment. I stroll in their shadow as if at the foot of the Tower of Babel. Even today, the sight of a still-unpacked box makes me nervous. They seem to harbour some malignant promise. Whenever I move house, I cram them spitefully into corners.

The lie has a simple, well-intentioned source: a deceptive manoeuvre for our less trustworthy acquaintances and for me, the unpredictable element, the child, whose ignorance has already caused harm. My grandmother Ada teaches a couple of Western foreign-exchange students and, once in a while, her favourite visits her at home. On one of these occasions, a toy, made in the USA out of real fur, is given to me. Within an hour I, Judas, break the promise to keep my mouth shut. Overwhelmed by this gift of aggressive capitalism, I gloat about it in front of the appreciative audience gathered there. As a result, the family is terrified for weeks. Risky private contact with foreigners quickly brings the suspicion of collaboration. That kind of notice reduces your chances of acquiring an exit visa to near zero. Our communal apartment is equipped with a chief spy in the reserves who has not recovered from being put into retirement and is, in any case, a fertile source for the most absurd reports to officials. Suffering agonies of stupefying meaninglessness, this Hero of Labour perches for hours in front of the communal telephone and transcribes into a file kept for just that purpose all of the conversations conducted unfazed right before his nose. He sits there in the half-dark and sweats moral responsibility to the fatherland from every gleaming pore.

I have my own sense of moral responsibility at the age of six and, following its call, or simply another destructive urge, I put it into action with my friend Lenka's energetic assistance.

Our communal apartment building houses not only lunatics, alcoholics and well-behaved people, from whom Lenka and I descend, but also an ageing, unregistered prostitute, Aunt Musja, who is officially in charge of coordinating the university's nude models. Hers is the small room next to the two in which our family lives. Lonely and childless, she satisfies her longings by often inviting us children in and handing out treats, accustomed as she is to sweetening her visitors' lives. We always enter her realm with a faint foreboding of Hansel and Gretel. We sense that she occupies a special position in the social hierarchy: barely tolerated, even though she's always very friendly. This can't be said of many others in our building.

Sometimes the manic-depressive woman in the room at the end of the hall throws all her furniture out of the window onto the street below, bellowing the entire time, and everyone carries it back up the next day in stoic silence. Sometimes the drunk in the small room next to the kitchen beats her son and then, following the pecking order, is beaten by her husband to bring her back to sense, and also often because the last wine bottle is empty. In our Armenian's room, no bigger than a broom cupboard, there are wild binges, to which the drunk is never invited since her voice is so shrill. Because of this, immigrants are often bad-mouthed in our communal kitchen. All five of us children in the building have fallen far from our trees and we adore him, the Armenian, not so much for his wobbly gait and his mood swings, and not because you can recognize him by his smell long before he makes it upstairs but because he works in a toy factory. The days after every drinking binge bring a repentant flood of presents for us children. The most alert among us often loiter by the front door to see if he's loaded down with bottles of vodka. That way we can better predict when the gift-giving will start. I won't even mention the forbidden zone, the three rooms in which our retired spy lives in Soviet luxury with his beautiful, fat wife and which all the residents quietly give a wide berth.

Aunt Musja's little room, on the other hand, is an intoxicating Aladdin's cave, crammed from floor to ceiling with presents from her gentlemen and with an air of petit-bourgeois comfort that is completely foreign to us. An 'Open sesame' and behind its portal are little crystal bowls of bonbons, piled on pastel-coloured plastic dishes filled with mysterious contents.

With acrylic-satin throw pillows on a canopy bed piled high with duvets. With crocheted doilies on every conceivable surface, with countless porcelain figures, with a cosy genuine fur rug, of which she is particularly proud and on which we are never allowed to set foot.

One fateful day, we're overcome with anarchy. Surprised by a cold rain and left to our own devices by the adults busy just trying to survive, we storm, unnoticed, into Aunt Musja's realm, whose lock we'd tinkered with for more than an hour, sweating with excitement.

With a reluctant *click*, the doors open onto the room and we enter, trembling, amazed at our own boldness.

Everything we have only been allowed to gaze at reverently without touching is now ours!

Hesitant at first, we're soon in a frenzy. We open jars, drawers, sweet boxes. We're quickly glutted with their contents and strew them over the bed and the floor. We knock over a shepherdess with her shepherd and shove the pile of shards under the bed.

The explosion of porcelain opens the gates of hell: what we'd so recently admired, we want to destroy.

Shouting and abandoning all caution, we roll around on the bed, throw the cushions until feathers fly and bounce on the creaking mattress up to the plastic chandelier.

I sit on the sacrosanct rug as Lenka grabs a corner and drags me across the parquet, sending the houseplants tumbling. Elated and breathless, we're surprised in the midst of our wreckage by Aunt Musja, whom, in our ecstasy, we hadn't heard coming. She lets her red-checked plastic bag slowly sink to the floor.

Something in it clinks.

She looks.

The orange-coloured curls around her face quiver like a cat's whiskers and then she lets loose; her shrieking freezes the marrow in our bones.

Denial is pointless. We're in the eye of the hurricane.

Screaming and skidding, we slide past her into the hallway. Lenka dashes round the corner and disappears.

I slink silently back to our rooms.

Hopefully Musja is too busy assessing the extent of the damage to see me.

I open the door to our main room and slip through.

Behind me, I already hear the click of her heels.

I disappear backwards on all fours behind my grandmother's massive desk, made of two carved, dark-stained towers with drawers, as massive as elephant legs, upon which rests a heavy wooden board covered with felt. On it, a lamp, its conical silver shade bent downwards, paints a patch of light on the floor and the piles of books. Luckily it's the only light in the room.

I cower in the corner, in the shadow of the right elephant leg, and hear how she tears the door open without knocking and stumbles in. I see her crooked, skinny legs two metres from me and hold my breath.

'Where is Mischka? Where is that little beast?' she screams.

Drawn by her shrill voice, other feet join hers. My father's corduroy legs pace slowly back and forth, always a metre from her, soon accompanied by my mother's calves in violet stockings, and the slightly slanted feet of my grandmother, the art historian, who, thanks to Communism, wears the exact same shoes as Aunt Musja. They get into a commotion, sometimes dancing by in pairs, sometimes alone. The shadows from their movements flicker across the ceiling.

I feel like Anti-Orpheus in the Underworld.

I can't turn round and can't call her name if I want to get out of here in one piece and, most importantly, alone.

The tango of complaint moves into the second room. They're looking for me!

I have only this one chance to escape; I seize it.

Back in the hallway, I'm momentarily at a loss: now where? I can't lock myself in the toilet, since we only have two for thirty people. They will collectively beat me to death if I stay in too long.

We only have one bathroom.

Anyway, the married couple who live in one room with the grandparents are probably shagging in it right now.

My heart beating in my throat, I approach my dubious hope: the only place that seems safe and where it's guaranteed no-one will follow me, the spy's apartment.

With the assurance of an innocent child, I enter the lion's den unannounced, and see, I'm welcomed very warmly. An opportunity like this doesn't present itself to him very often. No-one comes of their own will, especially not the suspicious child of suspect Jewish Non-Party Members. I'm served sweet tea and old cakes and smiled at benevolently. I'm sounded out masterfully, always with a smile, always calm.

If our foreign guest will also visit again? When?

American, isn't that right?

I don't know. I don't know whether I'm coming or going.

I sense a faint whiff of danger, but can't pin it to anything specific. The threat of the expected beating, on the other hand, prevails. I explain my reason for coming, but alter it somewhat out of shame. In my misery, I accuse Aunt Musja of having locked me in her room. I destroyed her room because that made me angry!

Oh, yes? How interesting.

Does she have money? What does her room look like?

Wrong question.

Better not think too clearly about how her room looks now.

I gaze into my tea in silent desperation.

The reflection of his small, not unintelligent piggy eyes swims there. He stands, bending over me, and leans his fat arm on the back of my chair, cutting off the way out to the hall. His eyes don't leave my face. I pull my head in like a turtle and am delighted to hear my father, the bravest of our family members, knocking violently on the door.

His outrage at my behaviour has given him even more courage to act. He, too, smiles cordially and drags me out of my prison by the collar. Relieved, I hang in his grip and am only too happy to trade the velvet limbo of that official no-man's land for the inescapable scene at home: Russia of the 1970s puts a lot of stock into black pedagogy.

The government's domestic policy also puts great store in black pedagogy.

Naïve, with long hair and bell-bottoms, small artists' groups with names that announce their agendas, like 'the Non-conformists', stumble from a heady mini-revolt into bigger troubles. The wide array of works, from the superb to the negligible, have a common denominator: the complete rejection of every precept of socialist realism. The first group exhibition offers a unique event that leads to inevitable disaster.

The public, bored with red-blooded peasant women and flag-waving heroes, pour into the show even before the opening. Sensationalist. The police officer, appointed guardian of public morals by the dithering city council, is overwhelmed by the bewildering number of viewers. In the hubbub, he loses the equanimity of a state apparatus representative and cracks down hard. Alarmed by his desperate whistles, a militia unit soon arrives on the scene to separate the onlookers from the artists. Contamination of the social body by the usual suspects must be obviated. Their worldview is known to be as contagious as measles. Quarantine is barely maintained by forcing the spectators into that half of the room, which has a metre-high wall topped with a small wrought-iron fence. The militia sweat, scream, whistle and almost end up unintentionally triggering mass panic. Because of the room's particular interior design, their call to order rings out as 'Viewers behind the fence; artists up against the wall!'

Not long after this, the organization is banned. Outraged and agitated, the artists meet in secret in their studios. Since these are not official communal apartments, the artists have the advantage of being able to choose who can live there. I'm often taken along to one of the studios, a dusty, smoke-filled basement vault.

An old wagon wheel with dripping wax candles emerges from the darkness of the ceiling. Gnawed bones of various lengths and thicknesses hang on ribbons tied to the wheel. I often glance up warily to measure them against the length of my forearm.

After all, my father had explained, his face dead serious, that we would be visiting a cannibal. He answered my hopeful question if other children would be there with a meaningful silence.

The studio's owner is a fat, bearded man, blustering and coarse. His thundering laughter echoes throughout the room, and he serves shashlik, grilled in the open fireplace, the fat sizzling in the flames. In counterbalance to his appearance he produces mannered fairy-tale illustrations filled with pastel-coloured landscapes. I don't trust his treacly pictures for an instant. He laughs and jokes incessantly. He is open to all guests and art lovers. With his intercession, my father gets his own nude model. Later, we find out he had informed on my father to the authorities. For the moment, however, the group frequents this studio less than others. Among the members' works you can find, in equal measure, the abstract and the absurd, kitsch and tedium.

They listen to the Beatles and try to tune in to American radio stations. The women paint their eyes as black as the abyss. They pass round banned samizdat literature. Samizdat is the Communist version of covert resistance. The free spirits stay up all night retyping page after page of works they will publish in this way. The banned books will be intricately smuggled over the border by revolutionaries and priests. And this is how the Bible ends up in the company of pornographic beatnik trash. Of course, father had already got copies of each and, to the great worry of my grandmother, who had some idea of her son's escapades, he stored them at home.

Fortunately, my father's sex appeal did not fail before his nude model, whose main profession was spying. She fell for him, very unprofessionally, and followed her physical disclosure with a verbal one.

Baba Sara, father's mother, had long had her eye on the girl. She developed the habit of surprising her oldest son in his studio, sometimes to bring him something to eat, other times to request his help with an urgent task – like screwing in the light bulb that had fallen out of its holder in the hallway. Sometimes it was just to remind him of his wife's charms. On one of these visits, she caught the girl leafing through his papers but could find no trace of the artist. The pretty girl was diligently filling in her notebook when the unexpected visitor exploded into the room. Outraged, my grandmother slammed the soup pot down on the wooden table. It had been clear to her for a long time, even though my father was still dismissing her warnings as prudishness.

She senses that her favourite son won't be with her much longer. She sets her jaw and decides to be brave and let her son pull away. None of us has experience with lifelong partings. She has no idea what she is letting herself in for.

She will never see him again.

This encounter of Lev's with the secret police is, incidentally, his first and presumably not his last. And the frequency of these encounters has nothing to do with his personal importance. It probably happens several times over the course of every Soviet citizen's life. The odds of these encounters happening are about the same as your average European's chances, according to certain Western statistics, of suffering from depression. You submit to the inevitable and simply hope to leave as harmless an impression as possible, if not actually an expedient or solicitous one. In certain rare cases, it is better not to make any impression whatsoever, and certainly not, God forbid, a good one. If, for example, you assume the risk of applying for an exit visa, then from that point on you'd better be as quiet as a mouse or as discreet as a toad under the bed. The system must not be able to find the slightest potential for a profitable alternative, not even for an instant and certainly not in relation to any kind of project. If such a project has any connection with the KGB, even if it is simply remodelling the toilets at one of their headquarters, then that is reason enough for a visa application to be denied. Anyone with 'skills relevant to the Soviet Union' is, for his lifetime, ineligible for emigration.

Before my father has devoted himself entirely to painting, when he was still running on the double track of interior design and work at his easel, he has another encounter with the secret police in the architectural bureau. A tall man in a grey suit, on whose breast insignia and medals in restrained colours form two handsome rows, enters the scene. The man is of an indeterminate age, with a smooth-shaven, well-groomed face, precisely trimmed, thick, white hair and a vigilant look. With this look he X-rays the entire staff, who stand breathlessly in front of their workspaces, wondering if this visit is a particularly fortunate one or will bring trouble.

The man, who doesn't need to introduce himself, inhales with relish the tension that fills the air and begins a leisurely round, pausing now and then to look over the architects' portfolios. He clears his throat meaningfully, selects a few of the portfolios, piles them on the office manager's desk and begins to look through them again. One of the employees can't bear the strained silence and lets out a sob. A colleague discreetly leads her outside.

My father has not moved from his spot. He observes that his portfolio has already earned an approving look and has been placed on the stack of chosen ones. He just needs to put two and two together. He thinks of the visa he is meant to pick up in three weeks, of the apartment he has already given up, of the significant smile on the face of the well-groomed man, who clearly has a contract to assign, one moreover that he considers a great honour, an honour that only an outright public enemy would decline.

He has no time to deliberate. There are only a few seconds before the visitor opens his mouth and announces the name. He rushes forward without thinking. Someone screams – probably the sensitive colleague. This time there's no-one willing to lead her outside. An outrage occurs.

The assembled personnel watch their popular colleague Lev as, gathering speed, he goes up to the white-haired man and lunges with his arm outstretched. The official's face suddenly contorts in alarm, and he takes a step back, just a small step, before his features smooth themselves out. In this world he is the lion, not the lamb.

Lev uses the momentum that has brought him so near his opponent and, to the groans of those watching, jabs his finger with full force into the man's stomach. The situation takes on an air of Punch and Judy – the visitor retreats in slow motion, holding his belly, while Lev, laughing and in the tone of a conquering gladiator, announces, 'No, really! I love this grandpa – I really do!'

The dumbfounded colleagues struggle to neither laugh nor cry. They try to look on as impassively as possible.

My father takes a deep breath.

Before he breathes out, the visitor puts his portfolio back on the pile, straightens his suit. His face is once again empty and calm, ordinary and focused. The secret service has no need for an unpredictable crackpot.

'Well, then,' he says. 'Well, then. It seems to me that this firm does not have any appropriate candidates.' And he turns and leaves the room again, although not without politely closing the door behind him.

My father runs to the toilet and collapses.

2

I AM THE CHIEF'S DAUGHTER. MY FATHER, LEV, IS THE OLDEST male in our family. I don't know of anyone who could be older or more important. I wait impatiently for the kingdom that has been promised me and for my prince, with whom I do not intend to share.

My grandfathers have both passed away. My father's brothers are younger than he, and Uncle Edward is rarely here. Something is not right between Edward and my mother, measurable in injured silences and reproachful glances. I can't get along with him.

Uncle Edward maintains his distance from his mother, Ada. With a wary eye, he measures the space that has been established between them, so that he can immediately retreat from the slightest lessening of that distance. Edward will be the first to follow us to the West. His way will be more arduous, taking him far across the ocean to the United States. But he is still careful to observe the obligatory celebrations – New Year's, birthdays and now our goodbye party. He sits there sullenly, his gaunt shoulders raised, hiding behind his beard and glasses, and remains silent. He has charged his wife with all the talking and she builds a protective wall of anecdotes and civilities around him. His children float around him like wiry satellites.

His withdrawal began in a hospital corridor in the dim light of a flickering lamp, when he was fidgeting on a folding metal chair and trying to stow his long, ungainly adolescent legs and his too-large shoes unobtrusively under his seat.

He looks up at the closed white glass door, behind which he hears steps, now and then a rustling, now and then the clink of metal instruments being set down.

He sits there alone.

It is late. He would gladly drop off on this uncomfortable chair, with his head against the chipped wall. At least a short break. His mother's fancy leather bag is thrown carelessly on the chair next to him. It is open, wallet, papers and fine gloves spilling out.

He is close to tears, but keeps a grip on himself for fear that a doctor might turn the corner and find this older boy fallen to pieces.

Once again he envies his half-sister her privilege of being allowed to stay home with a nanny and sleep.

For her part, she will envy him his exhausted endurance in the hospital her whole life. No, there will never be peace between the two. She will always remind him that he is left over, that he lost his father, while she stands there, with all the advantages of a late and long-desired child, and still wants him and his affection!

He listens for the soft voices behind the door.

He knows things look bad for his stepfather, of whom he is fond. He knows that they all ignored the serious illness for a long time, his stepfather himself, his mother and all the others, too.

Just the day before, he heard how his mother, cursing softly, had blamed herself. She will torture herself for a long time to come with the memory of these last weeks, will suffer from sleeplessness. The long vigil gives her the opportunity to torment herself with memories, to hear herself ridicule him on their walks when he can't keep up, to relive their merciless spats, which she, the tougher fighter, always wins, and her anger at his diminished functioning, his distractedness and exhaustion.

Igor. Not Israil.

The number is the word, and the word is knowledge
And knowledge is power.
Which father's daughter am I?

She feels dizzy and nauseous because it all reminds her of something else, much earlier, something much worse, whose shadow she sometimes feels brush past her and disappear into the darkness where she can't make it out.

I know what terrifies her.
It is hers, but she gave it to me.
And what I receive, I never give back.

The son feels her despair behind the thin wall that separates his room from theirs. That is why, quickly woken by his mother, he got up at night and accompanied her. In the taxi she clasped his small child's hand like a cane. As she stares out of the window, he fights the desire to pull his fingers out of her grip, since he would like to find support in her.

He's not sitting here for his stepfather.

Carefully, he takes the soft leather bag and puts it on his lap. Then it is silent behind the door.

The silence is louder than all the earlier sounds.

It surrounds him, creeps into his ears and clouds his vision. He sighs. He clears his throat to drown out the silence.

The door opens.

A doctor walks his mother out, leading her by the arm.

She holds something in her hands. A small, thin object than shines metallically when the lamplight falls on it. He squints and recognizes his stepfather's glasses.

He stands up, takes the bag and approaches his mother until he is next to the doctor, who waits, takes his supporting arm from her shoulders and retreats discreetly. The door that reveals a dim room closes behind him. The hallway is once again screened off and white.

The silence is unbroken. The boy turns back after the doctor.

He is alone with her.

She relaxes the fingers in which she had been gripping the glasses and squeezes his right hand again, until it hurts.

He knows he must escape if he considers his life worth anything.

The number is the word, and the word is knowledge, and knowledge is power.

He knows he is next.

I'm inclined to agree with him.

Uncle Edward seems to be afraid of Grandma Ada. As generous as he is with numbers, so sparing is he with words. His worktable stands in a darkened corner of his living room with modern furniture and heavy blue curtains. He sits there all day in the light of the desk lamp, hidden behind his books, tables and charts, and is not at all approachable. The ballerina and I slip past the living-room door; her brother usually stays in the park after school.

Mother often telephones her brother and is put off, but after a short time she tries to reach him again. He quickly hands the receiver to his wife, Olga. The atmosphere between him and Mother is always strained.

Aunt Olga is strict. Under her watchful eye my cousin performs gruelling exercises in front of the mirror. Her serious little face is sunk in the music and movement, with small but deep furrows between her eyebrows. The mother's chin goes up and down in time to the music. She has to force herself to stay in her chair and not join in the exercises with her daughter.

He will feel the same scrutinizing look upon him on the other side of the ocean. He should just turn and pirouette on the slippery parquet of American society. It will lovingly help him up, should he make a false step.

It will allow him a short rest, before it sends him back, with a determined push, for another round.

He had tried to escape this gentle firmness in Ada, only to accept all the more gratefully from his wife what he had refused from his mother. He constructed filigrees of numbers around himself. He bristles with equations as if with quills. He gazes up suspiciously, first into the Russian, then into the American sky.

The large amounts of money he will earn will not make him feel any more secure.

He will receive letters, first wounding, then wounded and finally pleading. His mother pines for him. There is nothing she wants more than to finally end this long silence, to overcome this terrible distance, this abyss that separates them. Her son seldom answers and even then very dismissively.

He knows why she is so devoted.

He knows the song of the two mermaids who want to tempt him lovingly into the deep and dark waters. He still gets chills down his now crooked back when he thinks of them and the pleading and desperate look in their by now weak and dull eyes.

He becomes hard.

He will not put at risk the freedom he has unexpectedly won.

He knows he was lucky and found a dullard who would stick it out in his stead.

The number is no longer his number.

I know nothing about the upcoming separation or about the second chance. We will only meet again after several years. I will sit on the beach under Italian palm trees, holding tightly closed against the November winds my red Tyrolean jacket we bought in Vienna and eating cold pizza with my cousin as the grown-ups, caught up in strained conversation, plough through the sand. But the reunion is short-lived. We revolve round each other in pairs as in a carefully constructed choreography that rarely brings us together. Her dancing takes her to a foreign land on another continent. Later, she will appear in New York in the Metropolitan Opera. Then she'll marry, won't dye her prematurely grey hair and will happily pack her *pointe* shoes away in a wardrobe. She will live with a Mexican in London.

Immigration is a tedious process with a contradictory – that is, an abrupt – beginning, like the outbreak of a disease or bearing a child. The emigrant takes off, like Lucky Hans, into the wide world but ends up in another fairy tale altogether. Russian fairy tales often begin with the malicious and powerful Koshchey the Deathless demanding his wish be fulfilled.

As with any terrorist, there are two ways to deal with him.

You can meet his demands, at which point something must be found as ransom, even though it is only described in the vaguest way with the motto 'Go seek I-know-not-where and bring me I-know-not-what.'

So you stand there and look. With luck, higher powers will intercede valiantly at just the right moment.

The second option is to kill Koshchey, an equally insurmountable ordeal. You must find and destroy his soul, which renders him immortal and which he keeps hidden in ever smaller animals or things, as in the ever smaller figures of a Matryoshka doll. Needless to say, after much trouble and turmoil, our hero will make the right choice.

That gives my parents hope.

But my grandmother Ada does not believe in fairy tales.

The world is impermanent, but not us.

We are immortal.

Time stands still.

The air around us is charged as before a storm and, desperately wishing for a clarifying outburst, I keep my lungs filled, ready for anything, but the all-clear never comes. Frozen solid. The imperishable family. Ice crystals coat our faces with a beguiling sheen; our toes, however, turn black. My grandmother leads our little troop as it heads, stunned, towards eternity and makes sure that we don't move an inch.

I am on the move with Grandma Ada. The scene is outside of time. I see myself with her in autumn as the enormous trees along the grey boulevards hurl their leaves at us on the salty wind that seems to come directly from the Gulf of Finland. I slide on the ice with her, dazzled by the glittering sunlight. The ice creaks and I bite into my frozen liverwurst, which sticks to my fingers, while she, wearing her light linen dress, leads me by the hand across the sun-warmed dust covering the boulevards of St Petersburg, her other hand holding her straw hat. And always, we're playing.

We play everything she has taught me: Russian fairy tales and classic literature, absurdly blended together and adapted by me into a predictable division of roles. I am the squirrel; she is Hercules. I am Margarita, the Master's lover; she is the big bad wolf. She is always the villain. For the sake of my education, she grits her teeth and plays along until I take it one step too far in a crowded Russian city bus – and when I say crowded, I mean it, my nose pressed into my neighbour's stomach from the pressure of all the bodies around me. Ada is playing Penelope, Odysseus' wife, while I am the loved one finally returned home, who hasn't yet identified himself, and I can't keep from asking the childish question of whether she, Penelope, hasn't completely worn herself out, what with all her suitors? My grandmother turns as red as the shining Kremlin star of ruby-coloured glass. Even the pickled war veteran across from us is curious. With forced cheerfulness, Ada declares, 'But please, it's all just child's play!'

I wander between the world of my childhood, the world of high culture and the proletarian world around me. Like Little Red Riding Hood, I have let myself be led astray. The contents of my basket rattle courageously.

Those who don't want to see must feel, they say.

They are wrong.

The number is the word, and the word is knowledge, and knowledge is power.

It takes three generations for secrets to push up to the surface.

They've already got rid of the second husband.

The old woman wanders through the apartment at night.

Small, frail, in a billowing, light blue nightdress.

Sleep avoids her.

Israil. No, Igor.

As soon as she lies down, she becomes agitated.

Lying down is dangerous.

If you lie down for too long, you may never get up again.

Israil. Igor.

Behind her closed eyelids blood-red shadows emerge. They move,

*trying to coalesce into concrete images. She doesn't need to be afraid;
that is why I'm here.*

Even if she has already forgotten.

Igor. Not Israil.

*Around three in the morning, she toasts her bread too long. She gnaws
at the unhealthy snack, propped up on a cushion in her room, while
outside, thick snowflakes fall through the darkness and she bends over
a dog-eared art book that sticks out far beyond her legs. On the wall
behind her, on which she leans her back, hangs a picture of the archangel
Michael, whom she confuses with the Evil One, Marx. His wings spread
comfortingly over her stubborn Jewish head.*

Which father's daughter?

The others sleep an uneasy sleep.

*The child lies between her parents, as does so much else they would
like to hush and to hide.*

The night is still long.

*The signalman's son decides to become an artist. He wants to study
painting. He has just turned fifteen. His father doesn't know where to
begin with such nonsense. The boy is apprenticed to a master carpenter.
He completes his training, pays with two fingers from his right hand,
earns his first money with wobbly stools and still wants to go to university. His father will accept architecture. He studies, builds houses and
wants to be a painter all the same.*

*All that his wife came by naturally, education and culture, her love
of beauty, he has had to fight for bitterly, just as he had to fight for his*

45

new life, the life of one who still was simply not good enough.

The coarse farm boy from the country.

He is obsessed with success; he wants to show everyone.

He is eager to climb higher and higher without having to sell himself. He is a dreamer. Dreams soar easily, but land badly.

The young woman is a fitting object of desire. He is always hungry enough to fight more, and to prove himself to her.

Nights, when the old one who disdains him pretends to be asleep, he paces back and forth in the bedroom between the television and the bed, like a pendulum, gnawing at nails bitten down to the quick and swinging his muscular arms as if trapped. His sleeping wife's sweet breath touches him lightly as he passes. He turns on the night-table lamp, feels the weight on his chest. The child shifts, murmuring, in the half-darkness. Her shadow profile, with its baby nose, paints itself on the wall like a nighthob. He runs and runs, but doesn't move from the spot. There is just the one path between the dining table and the bed. The desire for a cigarette tortures him. He opens the window a crack. Cold December wind whistles in and blows the column of smoke to shreds. He runs his hands roughly through his hair and over his beard. He presses his finger hard against his tear ducts. They won't release their contents, so he finally sits at the table, takes out a sketchbook and agitatedly fills page after page.

3

Not even pre-adolescent, I'm still in the luxury of childhood, sitting in an aeroplane to Vienna and am protected by ignorance of all that plagues the rest of my family: Grandmother by not knowing, Mother weakened by the illegal intrusion the day before our departure, Father crushed by the responsibility for the many steps he insisted on taking and then accomplished.

We approach the promised land; the aeroplane's nose lowers towards the milk and honey. Mortified, I vomit bits of schnitzel into the paper bag and lose my sense of hearing and sight. Armed with the two words I remember from my German classes – petrol and wolf – I descend from the aeroplane into the brave new world.

My mother gets lost with me in the elegant airport toilets. I am dazzled. We are herded together like sheep and led out under police protection. We sit in an old, stinking bus. Soldiers patrol outside. It's not clear if they are meant to protect us from something threatening out there or to protect the natives from us. I wonder what we could have done wrong. I can't think of anything. My mother is crying, and I can't ask her.

My father is arguing with another immigrant about our suitcase, which he left unattended for a minute. What little we have is a source of envy for those who have even less.

Grandmother Ada has got lost, so an energetic search operation is launched. She is finally found in the lavatory, touching up her lipstick. Why hadn't she told them? an official demands. She turns very slowly towards the men, at a loss for words. She thinks about her childhood German. Of course, it's rather outdated.

Ada's parents, owners of a fancy pastry shop on Lermontovsky Prospect in St Petersburg, had contemplated emigrating to Vienna even before the First World War. They had found her a German governess, a strict, gaunt young woman very critical of sweets and pastries.

It is difficult for the spoilt only child to get used to the woman's austere manner, her insistence on punctuality and unrelenting expectation of achievement.

The initial resistance soon turns to fascination with her lessons. The girl learns the German language and gets to know fairy tales from the Black Forest. She is particularly taken with 'The Cold Heart' and the idea of ripping one's heart from one's chest to find happiness. Illusory happiness, deceptive wishes and their fulfilment impress her. To rip one's heart out and trade it for frigid calm, for intransigence and rigidity. Her teacher's severity now strikes her as justified and reasonable, and she learns more from her than from all her previous governesses. It is soon clear to her that achievement can make you happy, even if your parents are unable to understand what you've achieved.

They are so intent on earning money for their move to Western Europe that they blindly trust the governess who is meant to prepare their child for the new world. Because neither her mother nor her father understand German, they cannot follow, much less appreciate her progress. Ada revels in a sense of power, in keeping a secret from her parents, in being able to step out of daily life and immerse herself in German books. Her parents rarely read. They are too practical. The bakery is their be-all and end-all.

The golden letters above the newly renovated entrance, 'Fine Confectionery', have been recently carved and are unveiled with as much emotion as Moses must have felt on Mount Sinai. The tables are of red and white marble, the chairs upholstered in blue, and the creamers made of fine porcelain, exquisitely painted, decorated with gold leaf and translucent when held up to the light. The counter with its brass shelving, by contrast, stands massive and majestic at the front of the shop. Behind it, her parents anxiously follow the political developments. No, no, it's not secure here in St Petersburg, the rumours spread. It's not secure here at all. Some distant acquaintances had emigrated to Vienna ten years earlier. That's worth remembering. It's really worth keeping that in mind.

Here Ada stands now, almost fifty years later. She stands in Vienna, before the cut-glass mirror that reminds her of the mirror in the sales room of the pastry shop, in front of which the cakes were displayed. She remembers the shelves decorated with small artworks of chocolate and confectionery, the starched ruching on the waitresses' aprons, the elegant ladies that met there for afternoon coffee or tea, and the imposing, custom-tailored jacket worn by her father, who had once been to Vienna to find suitable housing before the Revolution closed in on him. He had raved for a long time afterwards about the carriage ride through the centre of Vienna, a ride she herself would soon take.

Ada remembers it all, as she turns away from the mirror and faces the uniforms standing before her, impatient and incensed. She won't lose her nerve at the sight of them. She didn't then, and she certainly won't now.

Igor. Not Israil.

With dignity, she answered, 'Because I wasn't ready yet.'

The watchmen's faces take on an expression I know well from my father. This reassures me.

In the bus, my mother hisses at Ada, 'I can't believe it! Because of lipstick! They almost didn't take us with them!'

'They wouldn't have gone anywhere without me,' Ada answers regally.

'And why not?!'

'Because I simply wasn't ready.'

My mother sobs.

Father stares out of the window intently. The fire-spewing towers of the Schwechat refineries are still visible through the evening haze. The latticework of the metal scaffolding, wrapped in plumes of smoke, and above them clouds, in which birds surface now and then. The underside of the cloud mass glows, as if it had been dragged too close to the chimneys.

'Petrol,' he says to me, and winks.

I prick up my ears.

Now the only thing missing out there is a wolf.

'They have light industry here,' he announces like a specialist, even though he doesn't know the first thing about light industry.

I turn my head as far as I can from my mother's quivering shoulders and press my runny nose harder against the dirty window. Grandmother hands me a piece of toilet paper from her illegal lavatory visit as a handkerchief and makes the sign of the cross again. Behind us, our Jewish neighbours look vexed. My mother keeps weeping silently.

The sky looks the same as ever.

We wait in a long queue with other emigrants for allocation by the organization responsible for us. The queue is so long it spills out of the house in which the office is located and well into the garden, like an anaconda sticking out of a reptile house. We are so many, and our saviours so few.

Our goal is the shabby desk of the official who will interview us. The people on both sides of the desk are agitated. An endless wave of complaints washes over the man facing us with his questionnaires. There is no alphabet in the world that can capture this despair. Whatever gets set down on the form is not what makes up the person. Our Noah's Ark, which we've lined up by twos to enter, doesn't have enough room for us all; at least, that is the rumour. Whoever set this up was no friend of humanity.

No-one knows anything for certain, so every bit of information is passed down the queue, from head to tail, with the same result as a game of Chinese whispers.

I play among those waiting, sometimes in the bushes to the left, sometimes on the asphalt walkway to the right. The girl from our plane has landed with her parents some way ahead of us. The queue moves forward slowly and the space between us does not diminish. We watch each other from a distance, but stepping away from our families is unthinkable. She is as bored as I am, but is higher in the hierarchy of the waiting, right up near the entrance, and comes off as arrogant.

The many foreigners are worked up. The men are quick to argue. Conflicts flare throughout the overflowing garden. Culprits for the stultifying wait are easily found. A policeman with a plastic basket walks among those waiting, handing out cheese sandwiches. On religious grounds, there are none with sausage.

My first encounter with non-Communist dogma results in furious anger. What kind of country is this, where you can't get a sausage sandwich!

I hate cheese sandwiches.

Full-grown men are fighting over this.

I can't believe my eyes. I grab my sandwich tight and hide it under my jumper.

Sure is sure.

Later, when the butter has melted and run down the front of my dress, my mother stops weeping and starts screaming.

*

We are settled in a dubious hotel near the Gürtel, Vienna's second ring road, in the red-light district.

I spend my first days of Western freedom in solitary confinement. I'm not allowed to leave the room. We eat potatoes with butter from paper plates and, for the first time ever, fruit yoghurt.

'You'll love it,' my astonishingly well-informed mother promised in advance, when we were still in Russia and she told me about this wondrous yoghurt with fruit. I can feel this love taking root.

Nöm-Mix, the yoghurt brand, is the West's first herald I allow into my wide-open soul, even before the Barbie doll. I am reconciled with Austria. A world that produces such things cannot be bad. I was prepared to offer all my paltry native goods in exchange.

In the hotel corridor, I hear unmistakable sounds, screams, tussling and giggling. We lay there, naked in bed but puritanically covered to the tips of our noses, waiting until our underwear and the rest of the washing is dry again.

In the foyer, a bitch and her puppies doze in a foul-smelling dog basket. In unguarded moments, I slip up to them, lovesick, to hug them to my burning chest. In ardent longing, I bite my teeth together so hard that a chip breaks off one of my canines. I don't tell anyone, for fear of being reprimanded. I have too often watched my father pace up and down the room with a worried look on his face, rubbing his chest near his heart.

We don't know our way around either health insurance or doctors here. Next door, the battered hotel owner screams at her husband that he should go ahead and tarnish his soul with Galya, if that's what he wants.

She doesn't care. Couldn't care less. He should just go ahead. He'll see.

I find this new game entertaining and don't miss a beat.

The grown-ups see it differently.

Our books have arrived, but not the rest of our luggage.

The hit song 'A Purple-yellow Kangaroo' is playing on the radio. I reinterpret it bilingually – with a slight alteration it means, in perfect Russian, that a certain Julya ate a kangaroo.

We have stuck a stolen fir branch in a painted roll of toilet paper to celebrate New Year's, the most important day in religiously castrated Russia. It's enough for me. In the departure lounge, my cousin had pressed her doll, brand new and wet with tears, into my hands. For weeks I had been eaten up with jealousy and had quarrelled with her every time we met. My sense of amazement at the generosity of her gift still fits me like a glove. Next year, strengthened by a pact with my grandmother, I am going to demand we celebrate Christmas, and the following year, we will.

All the fairy-tale books in the world pale beside the night-time glory of Alserbach Street. What other place could so defy belief; I'm already in the Emerald City! It's unfortunate that I can't speak with anyone in the playground, but didn't words occasionally fail Alice, too? In the park, I build my own personal palace from sheets of exhaust-grey ice I've broken off the surface of the duck pond. I am Kai and the Snow Queen in one. My world splinters around me and I sit there, trying to reassemble the shards, but fail each time. The last shard sticks in my eye.

The February cold is familiar, but clambering about strange places is not yet. Undaunted, I storm the spider's web that is the jungle gym. Back on the strange grooved pavement, I watch the screeching crows, circling over our heads in the darkening sky. I follow their flight intently. The sound goes right through me. My grandmother puts on her thick lambskin collar and stamps her small feet in the snow. She watches the birds nostalgically, too.

Suddenly I feel I'm being watched.

The feeling is eerie and I quickly look around me. The bushes bend under the February wind. There is no-one in the park besides us.

It is too late, too cold for the natives, but it seems mild and light to us.

'We're migratory birds, Mama,' I explain over dinner in our dosshouse, 'and our letters are our cries.'

She doesn't smile.

She looks away and clears the paper plates we've been using for two weeks now. Father takes out his sketchbook, sharpens his charcoal pencil with a kitchen knife and loses himself in thought. We won't be able to speak to him for a long time now, even though he just sits on his bed, leaning against the wall, motionless and seemingly absent.

I sit at the cleared dining table, with a full stomach, and work on my crow caws. I'm writing to my lost love, Schenya from St Petersburg. I write about Vienna and fruit yoghurt. I put my last pieces of chewing gum into my letters. I paint St Stephen's Cathedral for him. I make him lists of funny-sounding German words. I miss him, as if someone had bitten off a large piece of my body, and I hold this first wound together, staunching the flow of memories. Before, we saw each other every day. First in nursery, then in school. A day without Schenya is strange and confusing. His serious, finely chiselled face comes to me when I'm asleep.

We're dancing at the New Year's ball, I in my white knitted dress that my mother embroidered with petals and he in a little suit with a revolting red tie. The silk bow in my hair slips off as we gallop and I let it stream behind me like a strange and narrow bridal veil. We laugh, all sweaty, and know that we are the most attractive couple in the room.

The black-and-white photo lies next to my pillow. He holds my hand, and I rest my pageboy haircut on his shoulder, complete with bewitching glance. A still from an old Hollywood movie.

'I love you more than my mama,' he says to me before I return to my parents.

Open arms wherever one looks; children are welcomed with pride. The cold weather and the vodka have contributed to the warm atmosphere. I run to my father's arms and look back to see Schenya rushing to his parents, and so am not looking at my father at all as he wraps me in his arms, which seem too strong to me, too big, not my type, not my size. Schenya doesn't turn round; his mother presses him, face-first, to her bosom, heaving under pink mohair. I can't even see his ears sticking out. She laughs, her head thrown back and red curls bouncing.

Her husband stands, detached, next to her and lets his eyes wander over those present until he catches mine. A look of disgust spreads over his face. Then he turns away and leaves the room.

I am confused.

Five days later, I'm pacing nervously back and forth in the entry of our communal apartment, until many of the neighbours want to chase me back into my parents' room. I'm in their way in that strategic intersection of kitchen, hall and stairs. There's always someone in a rush. The kiosk on the corner has fresh tennis shoes and *bubliki*, rock-hard mini-bagels you can break a tooth on if you don't soak them in sweet tea for a long time before trying to eat them.

Schenya and his mother were meant to have picked me up two hours ago to take me to the cinema, as we'd agreed at the New Year's party. I'm scared I won't hear the bell if I close our door, so I leave it open, until Ada starts yelling about the icy draught.

Frantic with impatience, I finally set out on my own when my parents are distracted. My mother wants to use the little free time she has to paint; my father had promised her he'd take care of my afternoon schedule. Now he's immersed in his own studies.

With a pounding heart, I slip my *valenkis* on by myself, put my two coats on, one over the other, push open the door with arms rigid in layers of cloth and run out into the street. The frost bites my face and momentarily takes my breath away. In winter, it gets dark around three thirty. I'm afraid of my own shadow, stretched out upon the snow, festively lit up by the streetlamps. The snow creaks under my feet.

Schenya lives two houses down. I rush up the stairs. My hair is glued to my forehead under my fur hat. The staircase smells of burnt meat, and the smell gets stronger as I get closer to the familiar green door. I beat on it impatiently with my hand, since no-one answers the doorbell right away, and I rattle the doorknob. I finally hear movement within the apartment; steps approach, large and heavy. The door opens a crack; the lock's chain stretches at the height of my nose. Behind it is the outline of a giant. I try to peer round him into the interior of the dark apartment. Schenya's father looks down at me from above. I take off my hat and breathe deeply. He still doesn't say anything. Somewhere in the apartment I hear a door slam. I look at him questioningly. He says, 'We're not doing anything today.'

I don't move from the spot; maybe I've just misunderstood.

Schenya appears behind him, as softly and quietly as an elf.

His father simply turns and walks away. Schenya's reddened eyes look at me strangely over the taut span of chain.

'What's going on?' I ask. 'Are you grounded?'

'No, I don't think so.' His voice was so soft that, even up close, I could barely hear it. 'I'm not allowed to play with Jews,' he says then, quiet and ashamed.

'So? Don't be sad,' I comfort him. 'We'll see the film tomorrow or the day after.'

It looks like he wants to add something, but can't find the words, even though he'd already worked them all out in his head. He opens his mouth. Helpless. He looks rather like a fish drying out.

Inside, a woman's voice calls him angrily, grandmother or mother. Lunch is ready. Schenya closes the door slowly. I stand there bewildered. I turn back to the stairway. I can't shake the feeling that I've slipped into an absurd story that concerns me in some mysterious way.

My cheeks red from the cold, I appear minutes later at my mother's easel.

'What are you doing here?' she asks me, confused, and presses the tip of a hair-thin paintbrush between her lips. 'I thought you were going to the cinema with Schenya?'

A purple stripe remains on her mouth like a seal.

'Not today. Schenya said he's not allowed to play with Jews,' I explain.

She puts the paintbrush down and looks at me carefully.

'Maybe we'll go on Saturday,' I go on blithely.

I pause briefly and examine her painting, a portrait of me she had started last week when I was ill. My captured second self has a swollen face and wears a colourful shawl around her shoulders and hand-knitted, flowered socks. The left sock is still sketched in, in grey and white, an airless space she is just beginning to breathe life into.

The heavy handmade paper is soaked and damp, the colours running, but she is still sitting there, waiting for me to speak.

'Who are Jews, actually?' I ask, as I stroke the coloured pencils arranged by shade so that they form a moving rainbow under my fingertips. 'I think I saw some on TV once. They have a very funny way of singing and dancing and slanted eyes like this, right?'

My mother puts the paintbrush away and sits up straight.

'No, honey,' she says firmly. 'The Jews, that's us.'

*

Now it is out. The dirty little secret.

The slanted eyes now make the child, even though she can't dance in a funny way at all. If she only knew what else was hidden in the fog of silence, in the adults' soundless understanding. The child still cannot connect the strange word to the strange experiences she has already had, and the adults will not share theirs with her.

Each one struggles alone and in silence. The small insults, the daily nuisances, the moments of real danger. The aggression is channelled inwards, towards those who bear the same taint.

The mother knows the friend's family better than her daughter does.

She knows what will happen. She is disgusted with the situation and with herself. Her child's naïvety provokes subliminal rage.

This potential future father-in-law is a good Party member who dozes through the district meetings on Wednesdays, Thursdays and Mondays. A portrait of Lenin in a small gold frame hangs over the sofa in his living room. His wife, however, comes from tainted family relations. Some uncle on her mother's side – or was it a cousin? – served time for political activities. The unfortunate young man had tried to receive American broadcasts. Now she must do everything possible to prove that she does not harbour the slightest doubt. She is a stalwart Soviet citizen, one who marches in the front row of the massive district parade, one who lays the biggest bouquet of carnations on the Lenin Monument, and, just to make sure the district leader has an unobstructed view of her doing so, she shoves a few competitors out of the way, women who no doubt also have some stain to wipe clean. They push forward fanatically as the brass band lets loose a festive wave of sound.

*

The girl writes stacks of letters. She wears entire pencils down to stubs, trying to convey a detailed picture of the West for the one she misses. She saves up the sweets slipped to her on the street by the sympathetic bourgeois, so that she can capture them between the lines, until the pages, colourfully decorated with layers of crumbled sugar, stick together. She hopes and can't wait; she knows that her friend will answer. Won't forget her, just as she carries his picture around with her so she won't lose the smallest part of him. She dreams of being able to visit him in the summer or, even better, him visiting her. The package of childish longing is sent off. The girl looks out hopefully at the lights of Vienna's Eighth District and waits. Her parents avoid her. They can guess the result of the letter-writing. Phone calls home are often cut off by surveillance officials if you do not speak clearly enough for them to follow the talk. It's also advisable to avoid foreign words in your conversation. As soon as the eavesdropper loses its general sense, the connection is severed. Those placing and those receiving the calls are careful to speak as slowly and simply as possible so that they can learn a little bit more about each other, but without giving anything away.

The fate of the letter, the one packed with drawings of churches and German words, is uncertain. The loved one won't receive even a scrap of paper from any package with Western stamps. Even if the letter were allowed through customs, it would founder on the obstacle of the patriotic mother. The tarnished woman will collect it from the post office and, cheeks as pale as a corpse, will trot home furtively through the March frost. She'll look around, to see if anyone is watching her, as if the treacherous envelope were shining through the imitation leather of her handbag. And she'll burn the whole pile of letters, with sweets and stickers, the whole

dangerous pile, which could destroy all her efforts in one stroke. She will
burn it in the bathtub because she wouldn't dare soil a rubbish bin with
it. Before her son gets home from school, she'll have aired the apartment
out for hours until the sharp odour of burnt chewing gum has dissipated.

'Do you know what longing is?' I ask my mother as I lie in wait
for her.

She closes the window. Outside, a mild Viennese evening falls.

'Well?' she laughs.

'Longing is when you love each other even though you're in
two different places.'

She suddenly hugs me so fiercely it frightens me.

I bridle and push her away. 'Like Orpheus and Eurydice.'

Mother pauses. 'They lost each other,' she then says curtly. 'For
ever.'

In the doorway she turns once more.

'But not Penelope and Odysseus!' I yell back triumphantly.

She frowns and leaves. I know better. Tomorrow, his letter will
certainly be here. Or the following evening. Next week.

I wait. At first, I'm relaxed, then anxious, finally beside myself.

I hover under my mother's feet when she goes to get the post,
like an alley cat, until she almost trips over me.

Mother avoids me. She doesn't look at me when I ask her about
Schenya. I'm furious with her because she gives me the feeling that
I'm searching for something bad, something forbidden.

After two months, I stop.

I stop waiting for the post. I don't talk about it, either.

Soon, I no longer write to anyone who stayed behind in Russia. After a while, I can go to the postbox without my heart pounding. I bring my parents their envelopes, turn away and let them read. I've lost interest.

Although there aren't any pogroms in the Soviet Union at this time, there is definitely a mood of anti-Semitism. It doesn't lead to fear for life or property, but it is palpable as more than a subliminal repression.

A slow poison, it surges between Russians and Russian Jews. The frustrated Soviet citizen is at the mercy of his leader, just as he was under the tsars. And, as in the time of the tsars, they need a scapegoat, a lightning rod for the public mood, someone to hold responsible for all their grievances, even though any display of religion has been forbidden for forty years.

The Jew, publicly blamed for the country's general misery, often has nothing that ties him to his origins aside from his last name and the entry 'Jew' on his passport.

Jews are blamed for political debacles, bad harvests, holidays that are too short and even for the fact that the vodka has run out again at the kiosk. An enormous country, in which many ethnic groups are united as Soviet citizens – another kind of melting pot – spits out the Schwarzes, the Blaus, the Grünbergs as useless. And they, helpless because they have no history, begin to retreat into their own community, just like every minority that is denied entry into a society.

*

The heavy curtains are drawn, the city lights kept out.

Passing cars paint roaming bands across the ceiling. The old wooden chair, with her clothes for the next day hung on its back, changes in that indefinite space between two worlds, in which it could, at any moment, begin to move and turn into a monster.

She holds her breath, so as not to wake it.

Her round cheek pressed onto her child's hand, she closes her eyes tight, until the darkness in the room melts into her dreams.

A carpet with changing streaks of colour, sometimes moving slowly, sometimes quickly. She thinks she can escape her past.

She slipped the picture that shows her dancing in his arms to her mother. And her mother put it carefully with the others in the cardboard box. Trapped fragments of the past. She is sad, but says nothing to her daughter. Her own loss runs too deep. The break was too sudden. It wounds her that her daughter must suffer the laws of Soviet reality even across the borders.

She knows her daughter has waited in vain.

She hopes she can grow into the new country.

Then, once again, she's tormented by the thought that it could close seamlessly around her and crush her.

The first letters with hints and warnings from pioneers in America start trickling in. A friend and colleague from St Petersburg urgently warns Father against following him if he wishes to keep living as an artist and painting.

Like old family silver, the golden West begins showing spots of tarnish.

My father attempts to make the humiliating wait for the Australian visa, our new goal, more bearable by devoting himself more concertedly to his painting. He paints on our beds since there is not enough space for him to paint on the floor. I inadvertently stage a spontaneous 'happening' in the best tradition of Viennese Actionism, by grabbing up a still-dripping painting. A complete transmutation: our fate corresponds to this incident – one quick move blurs all recognizable shapes. Everything is in motion and anything is possible.

My father magnanimously places heads and feet on the mess I created. The painting is sold. I insist on my share and reap scorn. Mother and Grandmother worry that I will become a barbarian in the interim and force me to practise reading and writing Russian. I find it a waste of time and consider the language irrelevant. Our arguments are legendary throughout the hotel. I evade potential beatings by hiding under the more valuable furniture in our dosshouse. My mother thwarts my plans by dousing me with water from a plastic vase.

In two weeks I get to know all the art museums in Vienna. My parents and my grandmother Ada are starving for new impressions. They expect a completely new horizon from the 'Freedom of Art'. I begin to hate the Old Masters. A winter landscape. A harvest festival and children's games. The Tower of Babel and its repercussions. Tired, bored, consoled only with raspberry juice from the drinks machines, I lounge on the leather-upholstered seating. My suffering gaze out of the window is returned severely by Maria Theresia.

The family worries that they will soon be shipped off to Italy or to America. They are ruthless and want to get to know this city as thoroughly as possible in their fashion. I would rather explore the parks and the flea markets. Just one fruit stand in the Naschmarkt with its many colours fascinates me more than an entire room of Brueghels. The olfactory enrichment is enormous; more than three-quarters of the goods displayed are unknown to me. The same heady excitement, the same zest for rummaging then sitting on the ground to devour whatever I've captured while I survey the passersby washes over me when I go there today. Here, it's easy to meet people at the sausage stands surrounded by junkies or at the market booths, most of them dating from the Secession and valuably supplemented with medium-sized pubs. I give walking the full mile of its length my best shot.

It's there that Father, unable to speak a word of German, gathers our first Viennese acquaintances together and organizes an exhibition for himself and my mother. Funnily enough, it is primarily leftist intellectuals who are interested in those who have been sprung from Communism. My parents take no pleasure in an attitude of rebelliousness. For them, being revolutionary meant getting hold of a smuggled copy of the Bible. They view their new popularity with amused consternation and boundless astonishment. According to their logic, our presence here should shake these Reds, who love getting together with my father, to the very foundation of their ideology. But this does not happen, nor will it.

The gallery seems splendid and the people in it very attractive, even the fat owner, who offers me a little golden elephant. When

I hold it tight in my fist, I can feel the soft, living warmth of the metal.

The gallery owner invites my father for a short holiday in his weekend house. For the first time I see a well-appointed child's room with an impressive collection of Barbies and porcelain dolls. Arranged in orderly rows, they stare at me like a hostile army, blue eyes under brown or blonde ringlets, grinning derisively like high-class prostitutes. I don't dare play with them. I accidentally knock one over and break her arm. My parents either don't notice this incident or mercifully decide to ignore it. An artificial lake spreads out before the veranda. The willows, covered in early spring fog, hang down into it. Together with us, everything is holding its breath. The snow surprises us with thick, oversized flakes. I burst outside screaming. I feel at home.

They indulge their cravings, take delight in nature, read and try to forget that this is merely an interval. A lovely house with a garden, with friendly, welcoming neighbours, with a well-supplied refrigerator. The weather is unusually mild.

Nearby, there is a ruined castle, which an artist friend has inherited. Invited by the curious owner, the family goes on an outing. A castle belonging not to the people, but to a single person is simply unheard of, a squandering of historical treasures.

An acquaintance of the family finds the tame ducks in the city park equally extravagant. If the West is not going to turn out to be the land of plenty, then at least he wants roast poultry. So he lies in wait for hours until he can finally get a trusting animal in his grip. He wrings its neck, plucks and cooks it in the tiny kitchen of the refugee housing. The result is as tough as his daily grind and brings him a host of unpleasant questions from his neighbours. The girl follows the trail of gleaming metallic-green feathers that lie strewn about the floor of the corridor. They are the same shimmering feathers she gathers with her grandmother as she dreams of being allowed to keep such a marvellous creature in the bathroom. In secret. The trail of feathers leads her, like Hansel and Gretel, to the scene of execution. The beautiful animals she admired in the park every day! The adults reveal their incomprehensible side once again. Crude. Ridiculous. Too much.

She is glad to have been able to leave the crowded housing for a brief time. In the posh country house, the ducks and their murderer are soon forgotten; too much flies, crawls and calls to her each day here in the garden and in the woods.

The wife's melancholy expression no longer changes; the husband prides himself on being the only one to see things clearly, which causes him night sweats and shooting pains in his chest. Then he lies silently next to his spouse, who, calmed by the touch of his warm skin, dreams of Paris and London, with her small hand on his heart. But even that does not ward off the pain. The old woman in the next room reads all night long.

Searching for suitable reading material, I rummage through a stack of hard-bound comic books. I torture my parents, who hate them, with pleas and explanations and interpretations. Ada condemns these cheap concoctions with an almost religious fervour. The only thing worse are hippies who fish cigarette butts out of rubbish bins. Even the peepshow she once wandered into by mistake is hardly more objectionable.

Walking through the city, they are surprised by a rainstorm. The pedestrians flee into underpasses or under awnings. Lured by red lights, which they still associate with Communist slogans, the three of them find themselves in front of just such an establishment. They have argued. The two women demonstratively remain at a distance from him. They turn their backs and ignore him, to make him feel his error. Now he stands apart and looks around in embarrassment. The establishment's bouncer thinks he is one of those bashful clients and motions him forward encouragingly. The man's good manners would never allow him to refuse an invitation. Curious, he follows the bouncer and is relieved to escape the reproachful silence.

Still, an argument between them cannot be so wounding as to justify a separation, however brief. In foreign lands, they are bound together by chains of fear.

Wherever the exiled one goes, the others will follow, noses in the air and eyes trained arrogantly above them. Yet their identity is so fragile, and the new homeland, which they must rebuild around them every day with reassurance, cannot withstand defection.

A traitor is not just a traitor, but a destroyer.

To the bouncer's surprise, two ladies follow the putative client – one of them uncertainly, the other determinedly, so determinedly, in fact, that she almost overtakes the man before stopping short in front of the first explicit poster.

There is a squeak.

The power play has shifted suddenly and unexpectedly.

The two women freeze.

The man stops before the glass case.

He gives the impression of being an art lover, marvelling at a museum exhibition. Now the two women must wait until he decides to leave. They will not move a step without him. He knows this too well not to use it to his advantage.

The bouncer stands in the centre of the entrance and considers whether he should lead the odd group deeper into the glowing red interior of his kingdom or had better usher them out immediately before their hesitation scares away other customers. The older woman clears her throat, half angrily, half choking. She takes off her glasses to protect herself from the surroundings and rolls them in her hands like a compass needle that uselessly points here and there. Her gaze is frozen on her son-in-law's face and, although he knows that instead of his features, she can only see a blurred surface, he lowers his eyes and begins to retreat.

My grandmother looks at me suspiciously, as I begin, early on, to fall under the sway of the West's drugs, then, wrinkling her nose, lays a copy of Dostoevsky next to my colourful pile of comics. We endure Donald and Mickey's American Dream without being able to understand it. Later, my father joins in.

'Look here,' he launches his campaign, 'just look how badly they've drawn the characters.'

I don't answer.

'The line work is not expressive.'

Mickey smiles at me conspiratorially.

I waver.

'The faces are stencilled in; they all only have one expression. They're all the same.'

Finally. All the same.

The good ones smile; all the bad ones have darker-tinted faces and stubble; that's good enough for me.

My father scratches his own dark-toned beard as he flips through the pages.

'But, Mischka, this is not art.'

He puts a sketchpad and pencil down right next to Ada's book, which I've already shoved to the side with my elbow.

I sigh heavily, pick them up and start drawing Mickey as soon as he leaves the room.

The opening of Father's show causes him a nightmare. In it, he wakes up in his underwear in their double bed, where strangely he seems to be alone, and suddenly he realizes he is on a podium in the middle of the gallery. But that is not it. President Carter appears out of nowhere, with a posse of journalists in a storm of flashbulbs. He examines the work on display, approaches the bed in the centre of the room and ominously asks my father about his profession. My father truthfully confirms that he is a painter.

President Carter is silent, sighs, scratches his chin and, just before disappearing, suggests an entirely new profession.

'You know, we also have completely different job options for immigrant artists in America – street cleaner, for instance.'

He wakes, covered in sweat and screaming that never in his life will he want to go to America. The show, honoured by a few mentions in the papers, is a success. My father sells several works and Laura sells two portraits. It changes our lives as unexpectedly as the blurred inks of the picture I had waved about.

We can stay.

Suddenly my father notices the similarities between Vienna and St Petersburg. He is already suffering from homesickness and will for the rest of his life. It whispers to him daily that here he is not that far from his loved ones at home. He will not return from his first visit to St Petersburg after the fall of the Iron Curtain.

I go to primary school here. In Russia, I had only had a taste of school for two weeks. As soon as the school was notified of our upcoming departure from Russia, I was branded a maggot on the healthy body of the people and was treated accordingly, so my mother decided to keep me at home until then. But it is clear that we will be staying in Austria for some time. I am eight years old and already behind.

Still, we learn how to survive.

So as not to lose any time, my parents stick me in second form in the middle of the school year, without the slightest idea about the language or anything else. The leap into cold water is assisted by a kick up the arse. (Later, I will declare that undergoing this kind of challenge is my favourite hobby.)

These students without uniforms immediately see I'm an outsider. Unlike the Turkish and the Yugoslavian children, however, I don't have a gang or a common language I can hide behind, but that makes me more exotic and gives me a higher social status.

Because I get colds easily, my mother ties a kerchief on my head, a disgrace that annihilates any social progress I had managed to make. I put every last bit of strength into quickly learning to speak German better than the others and use this to distance myself from them. Throughout my school years I bitterly despise minorities. I want to unload the contempt I feel for myself onto others as cheaply as possible.

I complain to my parents, plagued by the illusion that everyone here is very blonde, completely opposite to me. My ability to charm by playing the cultured little adult does not work here. I have to develop an entirely new strategy, but my appearance shipwrecks me before I even begin.

My first Austrian friend is sister to four other children and lives in the company of a dozen animals: dogs, cats and several budgerigars, all in fifty square metres. I do not understand that she is an exception and assume that the natives here are all passionate animal lovers.

4

WHEN I CLOSE MY EYES AND DIVE INTO THE RED DARKNESS behind my lids, I see them, unripe shadows roaming, large, small, vague shapes in the half-light, in the half-light of the first lonely morning or in the half-light of memory, as fluid and intangible as their bodies, scattered on the scrap heaps of the Roman outskirts.

Perhaps I hear them more clearly than I see them. I can hear the rustling of discarded paper under their searching muzzles, the crackle of plastic under their scrabbling paws. I can hear their fitful breathing, coming faster and faster in the unfamiliar Italian heat, but also out of despair and the enormous effort that comes with the stubborn and pointless attempt to find a way back. An impossible road to a place that no longer exists, beyond space and time, grown inaccessible and indistinct in the past, and when, with this realization, the first waves of sorrow reach me, tentative at first, gradually increasing, I understand the look in his eyes, when he told me about them, about the dogs of Ostia, which we, ourselves, are.

Dogs of Jewish émigrés, pure-blood and wild mixes brought from Russia, dogs that shared their masters' journeys through Vienna to Italy. The dogs belong to large families who had to leave much behind, but could not give them up. They are also the life companions of those who dare to go it alone. In leaving the Soviet Union, their owners forfeited all rights.

With that move, the animals became, like most other belongings or works of art, too, the property of the Communist state and had to be bought back, piece by piece. Possessions, however, were not all they surrendered when leaving that land. Usually one's passport was taken as well, for with the open betrayal of the ideal, one lost the right to be a member of that society. Not unlike a golem, whose vitality is fed by the parchment that is covered with signs and stuck in its mouth, the old, official identity, without its papers crumbled into dust.[1]

Without the magic writing and stamps, without any legal rights or entitlements, they sail, dog and owner, towards their uncertain future. The next border crossing clarifies the confusion somewhat: the dog, like its entourage, is issued its own stateless papers and becomes part of a cluster of refugees, housed in an area set aside just for them. In Vienna, they all still camp together, in quarantine.

Then I realize that I've been in Ostia once before. I ran through

1 This similarity goes further. Despondent émigrés who wished to return home set up tents in the snow outside the golden gate of the Soviet Embassy, in the vague hope of getting hold of a return visa, just as golems, when the parchment is removed, begin to fall apart and, in their disintegration, must return to their masters.

the grey foam of the November sea and ground between my fingers cold, hard clusters of dried seaweed, which were carried away like straw in the wind. I loved this rather desolate region, scattered with small bungalows, dilapidated, miserable, as colourless as the tedious morning I spent with my distracted cousin. And this shaped our parting for the next thirteen years. Her family followed mine, but strayed from the beaten path to Vienna. Before they could turn round, they found themselves suddenly washed out of Leningrad – which, just as suddenly, mutated into St Petersburg – and into the great Roman Empire, where now, in the damp Ostian wind, they remembered the Russian autumn, which would already have treated them to snow and ice.

We had come here again, to see them off to America. We remain like flotsam at the first watershed. My eyes, until then turned back towards Russia, find a new perspective: for everyone it's far, but for some it's even further.

It is complicated between us children, too. Together we sleep on the sofa and don't speak during the day; we avoid each other's eyes. As her long, dark hair blows in my face, we scrabble at the Italian sand, trying to find a handhold. I'm already well travelled and experienced. I've written off my two other cousins in Russia and won't hesitate to sacrifice this one as well. She, the beautiful prima ballerina, whose daily stretching exercises were meant to protect her from aching arms and legs, drilled and forced into shape in the forge of the Russian cadre, where she gave up her childhood at the age of four, is a constant source of envy. This perfect Snow White annoyed me from my earliest childhood, all

76

the more since I often felt her father's glance, measuring, annihilating, resting upon me.

They scurry past again, the dogs. They rummage and scrabble; they dig and scratch. They have no choice: they want to live. The most attractive among them, the ones with pedigree, will most likely be separated out and taken in by the Romans, who have figured out where they are abandoned. Entire groups make a pilgrimage every weekend, when the evacuations of immigrants are scheduled, out to the grey havens of the suburbs.

I'm a mutt. My dancing cousin will appear with Baryshnikov at the Metropolitan and I will land in a drunken horde of punks on Pilgram Street.

The next stage of the journey is Italy. Visa applicants wait here for their notification. There are only two destinations from here: Israel or America. Assistance from aid organizations is not as consistently and as tightly organized here as it is in Vienna.

Sooner or later, the money saved up for the trip runs short and many travellers are forced to give up everything that is not essential.

But the most essential is love.

So that they won't be separated from their dogs, they're willing to starve while they wait. Yet their wait can be extended indefinitely. Provisions cannot.

Even if they can hold out long enough, until they get their visa, they must still face the next disillusionment. For in each case, there is never enough money for an import licence to America. The animals, brought all the way to Rome with great effort, cannot,

77

under any circumstances, be taken with them. The desperate owners have no choice but to abandon them in the suburbs before their flight leaves.

So, every week, the area gets a surge of new life. In droves the dogs stream over the rubbish dumps and into backyards. They search for food, for their owners, for their homes. They wander around under the midday sun that throws the hard, clear shadows of their bodies onto the asphalt, dark shapes that rise again in my half-light only to expire, again and again, in fitful movements.

5

OUR APARTMENT COULD HAVE BEEN LIFTED RIGHT OUT OF St Petersburg and my family proudly insists on preserving all their Russian peculiarities. Like a bastion of Bolshevism, they defy the rules of the game in the new world, but they can't manage without my services as interpreter and guide.

Like Napoleon in the Russian winter, we are ready to sit it out and force the foreign land to its knees. The result of our efforts is predictable. I am straddling the gap ever more precariously. The continental tables, on each of which I have planted a leg, drift apart and I'm dismayed that I haven't mastered the splits.

From a distance, Grandmother Ada and my parents look with suspicion on my reconnaissance missions into the strange world. Ideally they would disinfect me each time I return to the apartment like a cosmonaut come back to earth. My insistence on a jean jacket with an E.T. decal horrifies them. I am twelve and look fifteen. My father, actually open and liberal, regresses to staunchest patriarchy. My budding femininity is destroying his illusion of a much-desired male heir, a role I had, until then, been able to fill.

All the freedom I'd previously been granted was washed away with my period. Suddenly I am no longer allowed to walk alone on the streets after eight in the evening. 'Respectable girls don't do that.' I'm stunned.

Freedom, they had always told me, is the greatest good. For freedom, no price can be too high. We sacrificed our homeland and our language for freedom. It was for freedom, Lev said, that he brought me here.

Enraged, I stand before the mirror and hear the key turn in the lock of the children's room door. Rapunzel had it better than I do. I hate the hair that is sprouting under my arms. Everyone must atone. I am locked in because of it. The dark fuzz on my pudenda is a harbinger of my failure. I should have been a ruler, an heir to the throne, a prince!

With a grimace of pain, I yank out a few of the longer hairs. I beat halfheartedly on my soft flesh. I am disgusted by these revolting mounds rudely blossoming out of my chest without giving a damn whether they're wanted or not, and I force them into my mother's old, worn-out bras.

With bated breath and the key ring in her hand, she stands in the hallway before the door, trying to hear what her daughter is getting up to in the room behind it. At the end of the short hallway, she also hears the man standing behind the bedroom door. The floorboards creak when he shifts his weight from one leg to the other.

She doesn't know if she should allay his jealousy, if her daughter should be allowed to do more than she herself is allowed. She counts the glances he throws after the blossoming girl and gathers them in the treasure chest of insults she has stored up.

At night, she hears his hushed, hoarse whisper next to her ear. It was all a mistake, a mistake! Soon their daughter will be out hanging around with good-for-nothings, tainting them, tainting everything. She will drain the honour from their very bones. She hugs him tentatively. He shakes off her cool hand, punches his pillow. She winces. And now that stupid music is droning out of their daughter's room again! She reminds him that it's the Beatles – he used to listen to them, too. Doesn't he remember? He is pig-headed. That's not the Beatles. It's rubbish.

His breath is awful. She wrinkles her nose. It is bitter and smells of smoke and old coffee. She turns over. His shaggy head appears at her shoulder. She waits a long time before saying it. Does he think their daughter is prettier than she is?

He suddenly jumps out of bed and storms off into the kitchen, slamming the doors behind him. He will sit there for hours, a cup of coffee in front of him, until the old woman, driven by other worries, disturbs his nocturnal meditation. She gives him a reproachful look, gets herself some coffee and sits silently across from him, until her mere presence chases him back to her daughter's bed.

Now the wife stands outside the door to the child's room. She represses the memory of the desperate sniffling in the bedroom and, holding the key like a magic wand, she listens for any noise from the two opponents who are concentrating on her from behind their closed doors. She doesn't even know what she should wish for and lets the key sink back down.

The child is unpredictable, a natural disaster. Soon her own beauty *could be supplanted, challenged, devastatingly criticized. She hears the girl swear; something falls and splinters. She winces and hopes it wasn't the mirror.*

My mother tears the door open with a jerk. I have just thrown a shoe into the wardrobe that is fastened on the wall. The blow knocks the mirror off the bracket and it shatters on the ground. I smile at her triumphantly: the door is open. I am standing in the middle of a disaster zone.

She looks sad and insulted. I want to comfort her and turn my nasty look away from her, down to the fragmented face, looking up at me from the floor.

She purses her lips and says, 'Now you'll have seven years' bad luck.'

It takes me a long time to realize the change is permanent. A dogged war is resumed. I have the weaker hand. I spend the next years locked in the tower of my burgeoning obesity at my easel or my typewriter, in strange spheres of complicated, fantastical novels that all feature heroes who have no parents. I cut off my hair, which had been the envy of all my classmates.

My classmates go swimming. When it's sunny, I sit in a darkened room, in damp underwear and type my ardour onto endless sheets of thermal paper. Just as earlier, my homeland and my land of immigration forced me into a balancing act, I am now walking a tightrope between the worlds of youth and adulthood. The scent of awakening sexuality is faint in my realm. I would rather not embark on this second emigration just yet. I don't dare make the jump and dig my claws in at the rim of childhood and, as little stones skitter down into the abyss, I wait for the helping hand that doesn't come. So I don't move, either. I can't move. Ecstasy would wash me far away from my family, we all know that – they know it and I know it. Pooling our strength, we push the lid down on the boiling pot and listen to the rumbling inside.

The child greedily stuffs chocolate into her mouth. Moist, sticky sweetness on her tongue. This is the only pleasure allowed her. This house does not tolerate pleasures.

The man has withdrawn from his wife. He sees the downfall coming and awaits it impatiently. She finds the pills he is meant to be taking hidden in the folds of his armchair. Suddenly he stops keeping his doctors' appointments.

More often now, she cries secretly at her dressing table, covered with pretty little things that watch her quietly, as does her reflection, which she looks for in every glassy surface. Then she takes paper and colours and finishes a melancholy self-portrait. She looks at this second face over her shoulder. When she sits before the mirror, this second face stays behind in the bedroom and looks reproachfully at the man when he comes home for a midday nap. I see her and her many faces that dance around them in a chaotic roundelay when they meet in the hallway of the enormous apartment, as if they wanted to fill the rooms with as many inhabitants as back in St Petersburg.

Life begins to lose its colour. Someone must have washed it on too hot a setting. It doesn't fit any more.

Between eruptions of genital despair and lofty speeches I use to charm adults, I fall into a dull listlessness and a paralyzing boredom I try to cure with orgies of eating. There are days whose only high point is going to the table three times.

In summer, my thighs chafe against each other until small, bad-smelling sores erupt. I can no longer wear dresses or skirts. I skilfully hide my most feminine parts with a veil of fat. I let an apron grow over my privates. I'm well behaved. I don't go out. I only wear trousers. The days when others looked at me with interest – looks I wasn't able to interpret at the time – are over. My nonchalance and macho air can still charm some girls, including those who would not put up with any competition. I find a friend, a girl with a plait and an arrogant little nose. A rising star in the constellation of my puberty. My blond *deus ex machina* fits my schema.

She pities me, to ennoble herself.

With calm disgust, she tells me about her grandmother, a Viennese Communist who fled National Socialism in the wrong direction: to Russia and 'The Internationale'. There she marries and has a son. The war starts soon after. Like many others of German origins, the newly integrated Soviet citizen is accused of espionage. What had been spared her under Stalin now overtakes her: her husband is executed as a collaborator. She is stuck in a transport to Siberia. There she serves almost fifteen years in a work camp. Her son stays behind in Moscow with relatives who take him in unwillingly. They could be punished for raising a half-German child spy.

The Viennese woman is a nurse. She tends the sick in the camp and eats their rations in secret. That is how she survives. When she sees her son seventeen years later, he greets her with furious animosity.

The son is lost.

Later, back in Vienna, she will keep food long past the expiration date. She knows the value of food. She will never throw bread away. After all, she saw people die for it.

Her granddaughter wrinkles her pretty snub-nose over the rancid sour cream and hard bread.

Her grandmother is very attached to her, she tells me. She is disgusted by the stale air in her apartment, but she still accepts the expensive shoes her grandmother buys her.

Her grandmother's living room is full of Russian books. I, too, am a residue of her story, like my friend's father's rudimentary Russian. As he lost his mother, so he lost his mother tongue.

Her father looks at me suspiciously: I am a disgusting remnant of his past, a bearer of the Soviet virus.

What does she want, following his daughter's every step?

I want to be adopted.

To finally be part of this country.

To wear, say and do the right things.

To toss bleached-blonde hair over a bony shoulder.

She wears jeans with knee patches and colourful plastic hair slides.

In an attempt to be like her, I desperately pour myself into hideous jeans. She's allowed to wear lip gloss.

She paints my green eyes with black until I look like a panda bear. Before I go home, I have to wash it all off.

We struggle with waterproof mascara and fuzzy cotton-wool balls. Concerned, my grandmother will ask me if I feel sick and I'll agree and I'm put to bed in the middle of the day. I am, in fact, not well. I am sick with desire and there is no medicine for it.

My friend does not have to deal with any of this. Her parents ask her, amused, if she has a date yet for the weekend they want to be away.

She listens to cool music and reads *Mademoiselle*.

She is not able to come up with her own ideas.

She doesn't know any of the books I'm interested in.

She has a loft bed made of wood.

'Good God, Mischka! Just stop being so complicated,' she says, and I inhale this message like clear air after a storm.

She makes fun of her father's quirks, a man who doesn't want to let the family out of his sight even for a moment.

And of her mother's fear of ageing.

She lends me her high-heeled boots that are two sizes too big for me.

I slip and slide behind her on the way to the ice-cream parlour.

Later, she will be a model.

Not long after that, she will be miserable as sin, withered and alone.

She will trade her red shoes for an old, dog-coloured cardigan.

But here, now, in the bright, glass-walled ice-cream parlour, we're in a good place. She cheers me up. We shovel down dumplings filled with raspberry sorbet and covered with poppy seeds, smear patterns of sauce round the white plates and complain about our mothers.

Hers is cold and beautiful, like my mother, but meaner.

While she is still battling the wicked queen, I have long ago hidden myself away in the forest of my excess weight, where I am hoping a helpful hunter will find me.

Mercilessly, she lists the signs of her mother's ageing. Here she finds a grey hair in her mother's dark hair; there it's the crow's feet on her face. In the evening, I imagine how she sneaks into the bathroom after her mother, examines her in the dim light and records her observations with scientific precision in her journals. Her mother, who senses the surgical look, stays out later than usual with her husband at night because she knows her daughter is afraid of being alone in the quiet apartment.

During the day, it's different. We're confident and strong.

Together we make for a perfect infernal duo.

We sit on the school wall and comb our long hair.

With her shining golden comb, she lures admirers, who founder on the cliffs of her narrow-mindedness.

My songs are unheeded.

My mother seems to have discovered a sadistic vein and dresses me in girlish clothes that are too tight. My sister won't be spared, either. But I am born to the art of sartorial warfare.

The dark Russian forest murmurs not far from our summer home, the shed next to a dacha that is firmly in the hands of a Party apparatchik. We live in a small wooden shack that looks more like a barn. Ada and Laura have furnished it as pleasantly as possible, with white, crocheted curtains on the windows and colourful counterpanes on the folding beds. When one strolls through the garden towards the beautifully carved fence, between blooming flowerbeds, one passes the magnificent building. In the morning, I have waltzed through the mud with the neighbour boy. We played revolutionaries. We imagine them to be something like glorified street kids.

Suddenly the landlord is bellowing from his veranda that I am sullying the renown of the great October revolution because I had – without realizing it – quoted war slogans. How else is anyone meant to know that I'm a revolutionary, who doesn't even shun the filth of the street, and not just some little pig? I answered the landlord, provoking him to a serious conversation with my parents.

The owner sits on this wooden veranda every day, sipping tea with homemade raspberry jam in the afternoon. In the evening, he drinks beer and then plays chess with my father since he can't find any other partners here. Then they sit together peacefully, looking at the dark violet sky, and blow smoke rings in the air.

Lev has gone fishing. I am out with Laura and we come upon a small clearing. Here it is unnaturally quiet. But not inside me. The blood is surging through the veins of my four-year-old body. The roaring in my ears is louder than the wind blowing in the treetops and through the overgrown ferns.

I stand up to my waist in high grasses, my left hand clenched in a fist, my right hand held flat. I am armed with a juicy bilberry of a thoroughly remarkable dimension. I am aiming at an unsuspecting target: my mother's delicate back, covered by her favourite white summer jacket with lavender pinstripes. It is a rare piece of clothing for Russia; she has treasured it carefully and worn it with pride for years. She kneels before me in the meadow, her back towards me as she eagerly gathers the fruits of the forest.

My insides boil with hatred. I can't remember what caused our quarrel. I don't even remember how it went. Time no longer exists. I am caught in a feeling of glassy rage, a Stone Age mosquito in amber. And arrow shot from the bow – no, a missile shot from a rocket with a pre-calculated course. The events unfold in slow motion. Sliding one foot in front of the other through the fresh grass, as if each were a hundredweight, I approach my prey. With a confident movement, my bilberry hand stretches out. As she turns towards me in surprise, I approach her and accomplish my mission. I press the berry with all the strength of my little thumb between her shoulder blades, as she watches me with widened, cherry-brown eyes. In seconds, a dark red spot spreads under my fingers, like a gunshot wound, as we still look at each other in stunned silence.

We are both overcome with bewilderment. Our eyes bore into each other. Then, finally, her voice, high and quickly breaking. She grabs me by the wrist, since I'm still there looking like a rascal and not saying anything, and drags me through the ferns towards the stream. She would much rather throw me in than the jacket.

Vengeance is mine, saith the Lord.

Mine is the sorrow of remorse.

I feel like a monster, a miscreant, unworthy. I would like to sacrifice my dearest wish – to fly – in order to undo the deed.

Mother's prized possession is lost, and with it my childish innocence.

The deflowering ritual is complete.

I have just entered the House of Sin.

I will stay here for a time, stranded in the waiting room and picking potatoes from the ashes of the purgatorial fire. Now I know that misdeeds precede deeds, that consequences precede acts.

This is the well I will sink into when my father dies.

I will have to return here to let the stone drop, and to listen to its silent fall for a very long time.

The jacket disappears into the wardrobe and never reappears.

But not my memories.

I felt the child's touch before her attack. Small children, the elderly, the sick and the insane are closer to me.

Yet I do not suffer from existence.

The woman banished the piece of clothing to the depths of her wardrobe. Sometimes she opens it, rummages around in the clothing until she feels the hook at the very back. At first, that is enough. Later, she has to pull it out and hang it over the clothing she has acquired in Vienna and which envelop her in her new existence. She sinks into the cloth's stripes until her eye falls on the rust-brown spot. She has not been able to fasten it round her still-slender waist for a long time now. She will throw it into the farthest corner of her wardrobe.

*

My mother sacrifices her artistic career and will make enamelled jewellery so that my father can be a painter. That will open a rift between them. We are engaged in a combat operation. We are at war with each other and, at the same time, with the outside world.

'They have stolen you,' my parents tell me.

The kidnapping is avenged upon the missing one.

I try as hard as I can. I have to deliver fresh-baked reasons to argue every day like still-warm Viennese breakfast rolls. Others fall to carving up their forearms with razor blades. At the moment, the good of the family is too important to me, so I create problems at school, passionate arguments that are celebrated up and down the apartment like a tango. I escape to the attic, barefoot and in my pyjamas, hoping to catch pneumonia, because I know, after a quick look out of the window, that I would never dare take a step further.

I am forgiven.

At the attic window, the stubborn cub sits between the dust and creaky old beams. Little bits of coloured plastic shine like ghost lights in the tarred roof sheeting. The tree in the courtyard sways with a gust of wind. She looks down at its crown. The rustling leaves wave like tiny hands grasping at emptiness. She sits between two storm fronts. She wants to go both forward and back.

Four floors below, her mother stands leaning against the window frame, looking at the same tree. Her shoulders are drawn up and she wears a sheer, frilled blouse and smudged violet on her eyelids. Both tremble on either end of the umbilical cord.

*

I have already changed schools twice and repeated my second year of secondary school. It doesn't stop there. I develop a new approach: I no longer want to be separated from anything, neither from destructive relationships nor from the curriculum.

I am redeemed from this school with Russian as a foreign language by changing to a conservative girls' school. The change moves me from the First to the Fourth District and spares me the social pressure. My shabby clothes no longer stand out.

My German gradually reaches the level of the top students. My cheekiness ensures me not only the title of teacher's pest, but also my classmates' admiration. The position of class 'bad boy', hitherto empty, falls to me.

I am now a miniature alpha-male and I take care of my harem. It provides me with study guides, sausage sandwiches, cocoa and affection. I am well taken care of in this female cosmos.

6

THE FEMALE COSMOS IS NOT NEW TO ME: MY TWO GRAND-mothers lead matriarchal dynasties. Baba Sara, my father's mother, just under five feet with a plait that reaches down to her hips and piercing blue eyes, is a closet chain-smoker. Her five children and countless grandchildren all pretend they know nothing of her vice. It would be too inappropriate. Baba Sara is a powerful alchemist in the kitchen, able to conjure up feasts from nothing, as in the fable of 'The Stone Soup'. She is uneducated and wise. I feel obligated to perpetuate her escape attempt into the world of art, cut short when she married at sixteen.

She quietly disappears from my life. For a time I can still remember the soft warmth of her hugs. She smells a little musty from spices and cigarettes. For years she has always worn the same kaftan with red roses. In the kaftan pockets, she not only has her cigarette packet, but her tarot cards, bound with a worn rubber band. Sometimes, in the evenings, she sits poring over the cards.

Her plait is undone. Her hair falls over her shoulders and down her back.

A cigarette smoulders next to her in a small silver dish. She nods as her fingers shuffle and deal the cards, putting them in motion and creating a moving landscape of images. A future, constantly changing, unfurled and unveiled, spread out on the plastic kitchen table in her apartment in the new housing development, while her plump daughter, Ljuba, her hair in curlers, dozes in front of the television. The moon shines through the perforated plastic curtains and rises above the factory smokestacks, bathed in red light, of this St Petersburg satellite city.

The Moon in the fourth house and the Fool next to the King of Swords.

She frowns and draws deeply on her cigarette until thin lines of smoke stream from her nose, as if she were a small, friendly dragon.

After our departure to the West, I flatly refuse to stay in contact with any of my relatives. I experience the loss of Baba Sara as a deep betrayal on her part. If I had been able to, I'd have peed in her bags like an offended cat.

Emigration tears people apart. They learn about high points and personal disasters in letters and phone calls. Closer contact is impossible. As if they had landed on another planet, breathing is difficult in the spacesuits they don't dare take off for fear there won't be enough air in the new atmosphere. Their chests rise and fall with difficulty. Their lungs hurt. The voices of the other settlers croak through the microphones in their helmets.

Her death cannot be verified. I know nothing of open graves or funeral wakes. I know people whose existence feeds only on voices over the telephone. Then the voices go silent.

When Baba Sara dies, my father weeps. I have never seen him cry before. He stands there, leaning against the door frame, holding the battered receiver, from which a busy signal has been sounding for a long time.

The tears trickle down the wrinkles of his face and into his beard. The receiver hovers halfway between his ear and his chest. Out of the earpiece comes Nathanael's voice, sounding unusually strong.

His brother, the tortoise, has overtaken him.

He was there when she died, when the hare was unfortunately impeded.

Father can only dream of taking part in Baba Sara's funeral.

The Iron Curtain does not recognize any final journeys or a son's duties.

The woman has brought me much discomfort. She shielded her son with her heart's instincts, her joy of life and her strength.

As long as she was around, I could not reach him.

Her time is limited. Mine is not.

When he leaves his mother and his homeland, I come one step closer. Now I've discovered a chink in his soul, into which I can set my hook.

At first, he defended himself, lost in dreams.

His daughter reminds him of his mother.

She has similar features, similar movements.

He clings to her likeness as if he wanted to use his daughter to conjure up his mother. He becomes furious when he can't do it. A strange world looks at him through the girl.

Foreignness edges in between him and his child.

He feels his power over his daughter wane. This horrifies him. She can no longer protect him.

He lashes out around him.

I wait.

Soon afterwards, a Jewish acquaintance appears and performs strange rituals with my father behind closed doors. I pace anxiously back and forth in front of the door.

Grandma Ada looks down her nose at the cantor, makes the sign of the cross and barricades herself in her room. I try to catch a glimpse of my father and the stranger through a crack in the door. The two of them stand, bent over their books. Suddenly my father looks up. His face has acquired shadows that make me duck down. He glances searchingly into the void.

For days he refuses to speak with anyone.

Grandma Ada avoids my father. She critically examines the Jewish bond that ties the others. Hers has long been broken. She has become friends with atheist Jewish intellectuals and goes to St Stephen's Cathedral every Sunday. She would have gone to church in St Petersburg, if she had had the opportunity, but at that time Russian churches were locked up or had been converted into libraries or youth centres. So there was nothing she could do, except set out postcards of famous icons in the name of aesthetic interest and educational value. She had pinned an enormous exhibition poster with the face of the archangel Michael over her bed. St Isaac's Cathedral, St Stephen's, Maria am Gestade Church;

Orthodox or Catholic, it makes no difference. A church is a church; a cross, a cross. Anything is better than the Star of David. But she will not let herself be baptized. She refuses to comply with rituals.

Grandma Ada wrinkles her nose.

After the family's first meal with her son-in-law, Lev, she decides to decline politely any further meetings. Her new relations cook a lot and use too much fat. They eat a lot, talk a lot and aren't even embarrassed to speak Yiddish openly – a language that no reasonable man, and certainly not a literary one, would ever be caught speaking! And even if she does understand some of the words, she would never let it show. Ada grimaces, as if some awful-smelling thing were being carried past her.

Lev's sister, Ljuba, is too fat. Her children work hard, but intellectually, they are nothing to talk about. Lev's mother goes so far as to force Ada into a hug. And she's wearing a kaftan, in broad daylight and in front of guests! She laughs too loud and shows her badly cared-for teeth. She smells of smoke.

Ada straightens the dove-grey collar of her suit jacket to wipe away the touch of those fat little fingers. When they want to exchange recipes with her, there is nothing but silence.

Of course, Baba Sara has not read Dostoevsky and doesn't know Schubert. When she does go to the theatre, it's only to see revues. She even wanted to be a soubrette when she was younger! Disgraceful.

Naturally, Ada generously accepts that Sara has only recently arrived from the countryside and was hardly exposed to culture.

Still, she wrinkles her nose. Her daughter has, on the whole, made a bad choice. She doesn't see why she should have to hide her opinion behind polite clichés. Intelligence and high culture aren't just handed out. She could have become the manager of a pastry shop, or worse, just a baker after her parents lost all they had in the Revolution, including the family business.

But she aims high. She graduated with distinction and immediately enrolled in university. She wants to be the best of the best. So, bent over her books, she studies through the night. Praise, she thinks, won't be long in coming. But she's mistaken. She trusts the wrong colleague. She talks too much about herself, about her mother, about her past.

She shakes off the shame of being publicly sent down from university because a fellow student denounced her as the daughter of a wealthy property owner. She weeps in secret. A week later, she counterattacks wearing make-up and chic clothes. She can still remember very clearly the sound of her high heels on the asphalt of the institute's driveway. With testimonials under her arm and lips painted red, she unleashes a storm in the director's office. She demands and she begs until, against all protocol, the college doors are opened to her again.

She did it with her own willpower and is now a university professor and author of several scholarly books. A model for young students, who often even come to her house to visit.

What is past will remain behind.
No-one will force her to return.

Not even via detours.

Even if the price is her daughter's marriage.

Igor. Not Israil.

Igor. Basta.

No-one speaks Yiddish but Baba Sara, so I don't learn a single word of Yiddish, either. Grandma Ada sometimes takes me along to St Stephen's, where I steal candles while she kneels on the little bench before the picture of the Virgin Mary. The glowing red window under the organ bathes the room in surreal light. She sits there, murmuring. She is absent. I look around. The powerful organ pipes loom up into the half-shadow of the vaulted ceiling like a demon's wings. The smell of incense is making me dizzy and wakens memories of Aunt Musja's perfume.

'Play with me,' I demand, after I've burnt my sticky fingers on a guttering candle.

She waves me off, like a pesky fly. I'm afraid that she has seen my deplorable behaviour out of the corner of her eye.

Now Ada envies the dead Baba Sara for the strong bond between her and her son. Every two weeks, Grandma Ada sends letters to America and gets no answer. Her daily phone calls are not accepted. To make sure her letters don't get lost, she goes to the Western station every evening so that she can personally deliver her airmail letters to the main post office. It doesn't do her any good to be in the open Western sphere. The wall between her and her son still stands.

Both grandmothers were elemental forces.
I am the child of two permanent children.
I am supposed to grow up.

7

THERE IS A HERO FROM RUSSIAN MYTHOLOGY WHO PLANTS beetroot fields with poisonous dragon's teeth, from which shadow warriors grow at night, one hero who always gets the princess, and one who sits on his stove, killing time every day. He travels on the stove through the village to the tsar's court, because he is too lazy to get up, and on top of that, he slays the dragon. He is the farmer's youngest son, Ivan the fool.

My little sister is born.

While my mother lies in the maternity ward, my father and I tramp through the Wienerwald. I am still the absolute heir, eagerly following the tsar, and because of that, I'm allowed, now and then, to hold the imperial orb.

We're standing at a wooden railing that separates us from a herd of goats – small, round animals scrambling nimbly on the rocks despite their remarkable girth. I look at their glowing yellow eyes under their curved horns, holding our stale bread tight like a treasure. As soon as I throw it to them, the animals push each other out of the way, their hooves clicking on the asphalt like high–

heeled shoes. Two of the goats are almost twice as wide as the others, their sides stretched almost to bursting, two little helium balloons with tiny beards.

'Are they pregnant, too?' I ask my father.

'Yes,' he supposes.

'I thought so. They're much more aggressive than the others.'

My father doesn't laugh. He becomes immersed in the striped pupils of the billy goat before him, almost at his own eye level when it suddenly rears up on its hind legs. Later, I will recognize the black muzzle and the grey stripes of the unruly pelt in one of my father's paintings that, even as an adolescent, I found frightening.

The horns and the empty eyes look satanic. The goat face, with its combination of animal and human traits, without a neck or a body, fading into the shadows, a husk waiting to be filled.

The long silence is becoming awkward.

I scatter the rest of the bread in one sweep.

'Save some for me,' my father suddenly says as I drop the last few crumbs.

I look at him without understanding. 'Are you still hungry?'

He bursts out laughing. 'Is it all gone?'

'Yes.'

'Then we'll buy some bread in the restaurant.' He sounds like he won't put up with any objections.

'What for?'

He doesn't answer and turns away from me.

I know there is a pub deep inside the park and that we've got a long walk along the boulevard ahead of us.

'I want to feed the goats again, too,' he says softly. His voice sounds brittle. 'Come on, Mischka.'

I sit demonstratively down on one of the wooden benches and scrape my shoes on the dirt road.

'Mischka, you lazybones. I'll tell you a story on the way. About goats and people.'

I follow him.

'About a boy.'

'And?'

'Yes, about a boy who had a hedgehog, a piglet and a goat.'

I catch up. 'What was that?'

'A boy who lived in the country. He was meant to become a farmer or a carpenter, like his parents.'

We stroll along the boulevard.

'It was me. I'm talking about myself.'

The sun is shining straight down on our heads. We still have the day before us.

We go deeper and deeper into the cool realm of Vienna's Lainzer Tiergarten and into Lev's past, step by step away from my childhood and towards his.

Until just then, I had never given a moment's thought to his childhood, to what he had done before he became my father. For me, he only exists from the time he was called to this demanding role.

I learn that, unlike my mother and me, who were born in the shadows of St Petersburg's cathedrals and palaces, he grew up in a small village on the outskirts – a hamlet that was gradually swallowed by the growing city. A proper little village, in which the residents grew vegetables in their own gardens and kept small domestic animals in their backyards. His father has worked his way up to stationmaster, a position he is proud of, since it enables him to feed his wife and five children. I learn that my father is not Baba Sara's first-born son.

The older brother drowned in a pond when he was ten years old.

Lev takes over his older brother's position and his job as the village's goatherd.

I reflect uncomfortably that I, also, am becoming an older sister today. He is so absorbed in his storytelling that I can no longer detect his nervousness.

So then, the village goats. The young Lev spends the entire summer taking a little herd from one small pasture ground to another and making sure that none of them, God forbid, wander onto the train tracks. He loves to stare into their glowing eyes, which remind him of mythical creatures. Their horns, twisted and bony, slide under his fingers when he strokes them. But he can treat them differently, too. He carries a stick, which the stubborn ones feel now and again. In the evening, Sara milks the three goats that belong to his family. The pungent smell and the warmth that flood towards him when he approaches his mother sitting on a stool next to the animals promises delicious food later that evening or for the next day's lunch.

'Rozka! Verka! Satan!' he yells when he sets out in the morning with cheese, a water bottle and a sketchpad in his bag.

This is the time that, aside from the goats, belongs only to him.

As the heat slowly brews up over the fields, he lies in the grass and draws his countless models, one goat portrait after another. Brown-spotted, short-horned, with soft, dark eyes and light, penetrating pupils. Long beards and bald heads, with curved horns, shaggy eyebrows and smooth foreheads. A catalogue of different physiognomies that would have done credit to Franz Xaver Messerschmidt. Sceptical and trusting. All of them, the old worn-out ones and the cheeky young ones. At some point, he sinks down onto the field, lulled by the sun's warmth on his tanned skin. From time to time the occasional passing train whistles in the distance.

Summer bowls him over.

A piercing whistle wakes him.

It is surprisingly quiet all around him.

Quiet. Too quiet.

As he is still sleepily looking at the grass, he realizes that, aside from the train whistle and the hum of flying insects, he cannot hear a single sound.

No bleating. No rustling in the grass.

He bolts upright.

The pencil falls off his stomach and disappears in the grass.

Satan is the oldest goat in the herd, a sedate, shaggy old ram with watery eyes that give him a tragic air.

These sad eyes meet the boy's as soon as he stands up and, as he looks around, he quickly realizes that Satan's sad eyes are the only ones looking at him.

Whether that sadness comes from being left all alone or from being simply too old and frail to take off with the rest of the goats will never be determined.

The other goats' whereabouts seems to Lev a much more pressing matter.

His heart racing, he springs up, ties Satan to a tree trunk and hunts all over the slightly sloping meadow. He stands in flowers up to his hips and sees not a single animal far and wide. He yells his heart out. Satan eagerly follows suit.

He lures them with every conceivable promise. Delicacies, water, lush meadows. At some point, he starts to threaten them. They will pay! Each one! Disgusting vermin!

He fights off tears. What will Mother say?

Her weeping is even worse than his father's blows.

He leaves the meadow to the deafening bleats of the ram he is dragging behind him on the rope. The hoof prints of the goats he was in charge of can still be clearly seen on the dusty road. Calling, pleading, threatening, he runs down the street that leads to town.

From a distance, he can make out a group of people.

From behind them, he hears halfhearted bleating.

His pace becomes slower and slower. A crowd of people are standing at the intersection. A figure has already detached itself from the group and comes quickly towards him: his father.

The dialogue opens with a resounding slap.

'Bloody idiot!'

'Do you have them? They aren't on the tracks, are they?'

'They're all stuck, you dolt.'

The story is as short as it is tragic. Between blows, the rest is easily filled in. After the goats left the meadow, they followed the path back to the village out of sheer habit. However, they took a short detour before reaching the main square, down a street that had just been tarred – one of the big city's first harbingers. They feel the brisk winds of freedom on their muzzles as the ground hardens around their hooves.

By the time the first villagers show up, it is much too late.

The owners desperately try to free their livestock from the street surface, but this proves impossible without a hammer drill. After much toing and froing, one is found. The noise goes straight to the marrow, and two of the goats do not survive.

Lev is fortunate within his misfortune and can bring his two escapees home. His mother spends the entire evening cleaning their legs while his father paces gravely back and forth in the room.

The scandal lasts a long time and brings the family into financial difficulty since the owners of the dead animals must be compensated. The reproaches continue well into the following year. Lev vows never to be inattentive again and especially not towards anyone entrusted to him. Never again.

I'm speechless. My father makes mistakes. In fact, my father failed completely! Time has sped by. We are already on the way back.

He whistles to himself, which he forbids me to do at home out of superstition. Whistling inside brings permanent poverty. 'Money disappears with every whistle,' he says.

We're standing at the goat pen again.

My father smiles.

'You see, only the useless old Satan is left when you don't pay attention,' he says as he throws the bread into the pen.

The goats press together like a brown and black rug. For a while all you can hear is their jostling.

'I want the pregnant ones to get extra,' I beg. 'They need more than the others.'

My father looks in his bag, which is empty and remains so.

Then he breathes deeply. His face becomes serious again, then immediately concerned.

'Come on, let's go home,' he says. 'Otherwise Mama can't call us.'

And so we drive home in silence.

While my mother is in labour, we fill our bellies with cherries we bought from an allotment garden. The eagerly awaited call still doesn't come and I'm allowed to watch television late into the night, as my father hysterically circles the telephone. My grandmother has stayed at the hospital with my mother.

She sits by the hospital bed. She holds her daughter's hand. The old woman doesn't speak. She is directing all her strength to her hand in which she clutches her daughter's fingers. She prays silently. Time expands and they are trapped in a bubble. An hour passes, and the next, then a third. The woman in labour calls for a doctor, awkwardly; the words don't fit in her mouth. They mix themselves up, scatter half formed and lose their meaning before they've even left her tongue. She raises her voice; she begs, yells. Her mother urges her not to be excessive. One mustn't be too bold, too assertive in a foreign land. It's dangerous.

The nurse criticizes the inadequate German of the patient who writhes in the hospital bed, her forehead covered with sweat, and leaves the room. The woman succumbs to an inchoate pain that grips her tightly.

She senses a whiff of danger. She knows she needs help, yet her mother is building a wall between her and the outside world.

Only when the level of screams hit her where she wants to be invulnerable does she stand up, drop her daughter's hand and leave the room. She roams up and down the corridor, stands at the window and looks at the trees outside, bending in the hot summer wind.

The doctor finally shows up hours later.

First, I feel excitement over my father's tears of joy, as he telephones half of Russia and, his voice breaking, bellows the name Magdalena again and again into the receiver. This is followed by blind rage and my mother's look, full of foreboding, as she waves to me a few days after the birth from the maternity-ward window. This cube-headed thing, peering out from its quilted blanket and howling, steals all the attention from me.

My parents' relationship is in tatters and my sister is a half-baked attempt to put everything back together and to rights. I am not suitable for that. My presence fuels their quarrels. I had set myself up nicely as the baby of the family and am not eager to give up my place.

There is a picture of Magdalena and me in which I'm holding her, apparently lovingly, but with a murderous, Medea-like expression. Like many others, this picture will disappear. We create images so we can ban them.

*

We sit in a Caucasian chalk circle and paint.

Each of us has an easel or drawing pad; the charcoal pencils rasp over the raw paper. We are deep in concentration and alert. We watch each other closely. Silence encloses us like a bell jar. No-one leaves the ring, so as not to break it.

Grandma Ada watches us, looks over our shoulders.

However, the arbitrator is partisan.

We all know it, but no-one says it.

We draw lines, shade areas into darkness, bring surfaces forward, hide things. Ada, the art historian, will critique our work. Mother's elegant, sketchy portraits celebrate the fleeting beauty of the moment. Her figures' eyes are expressive, unnaturally large.

Father is developing his veiled, empty mask faces.

Sometimes they have eye-slits behind which dark hollows yawn; sometimes he dispenses with playful details and leaves the face white, like a crater-strewn egg, expressionless and dead, beyond time. He calls one of his figures Torero. It wears a suit drawn in sanguine and strips of cloth on its head, some of them flowing loosely, some wrapped tight. When asked why a bull-fighter would cover his face, he answers curtly, 'Because he is afraid of the beast.'

The bull is death.

Out of that same fear, I exhaust myself in reams of the same figure, frozen in different motion sequences. Half designs for children's bed linens, half storyboard or comic strip, the figure of a girl in a red dress runs, bends and stretches tirelessly in the airless space, trying to overcome the white page with its hard edges at last and jump free.

The youngest looks farthest.

The youngest knows the number.

Uncertain steps, confident glance.

She moves through a world that is always two dancing sidesteps from the others' world. She pokes her head into their spaces, looks around, amazed, and carefully returns to her own domain.

She knows too much.

Which father's daughter?

The number is the word, and the word is knowledge, and knowledge is power.

The words that she hears connect two worlds and separate them again.

The language of the house is not the language of the street.

It is hard for her to find her way.

Words are confusing. She relies on her surroundings. The dark apartment with its high ceilings in which steps echo and a thick layer of dust on the splintered picture frames, the many pictures, the silence. The darkness of the walls, the fog that flows through the rooms and thickens as it rises, as if a storm that will never break were gathering under the chandelier. In the twilight, something seems to move, alert, hungry. She feels its breath when it moves languidly from one room to the next. Like a magnetic field. The hairs on her arm stand up and lean in its direction as it passes.

At first she avoids him.

Soon they tolerate each other in the same room. She avoids looking up, up to where I am calmly looking down. Suddenly the stiff hairs are frightening her and she reaches for the scissors. Her movements are clumsy. She wants to cut the hairs off, to cut them out; she cuts away and cuts into her skin, her flesh. Staunching the many small cuts falls to the mother, who swears quietly and weeps loudly. She moves everything sharp up high, out of reach.

The mother doesn't understand.

It's not done by hiding the scissors. The child knows it.

The mother is watched as she stands unsteadily on the ladder. She cannot reach the highest shelf. She is afraid of heights and stretches up, trembling, reaching for the box with her fingertips.

The mother is being watched.

They are all being watched and the one watching them hides in the shadows. My knowledge is the word; the child's is kept in silence.

One evening, I sneak up to my sister's bed and stick a howling vacuum cleaner under the covers. I want to make her disappear from my world like the sweepings on the floor. The thought of using a pillow strikes me as in bad taste. Originality is important to me. Her long face grows longer. She takes a surprising amount of time to draw her breath and let loose. The piercing scream sends me fleeing with the *corpus delicti* into the foyer, where I cower half the night holding tight to the nozzle. Hours later, I can still hear her whimpering and my mother's soothing coos.

My sister's arrival divides the family into two camps. My mother favours my sister, who is closer to her now and satisfies her need for closeness. My father decides in my favour. We have a common enemy: we unite against the mother-child dyad. Why should we bother with gentle bonding? Men don't have time for such childishness. We are bound in our search for truth in art and agonizing jealousy. Grandma Ada, who, up to his death only addressed my father formally, takes my mother's side and tips the entire system.

She makes an exception for me.

I am and remain her favourite grandchild, especially once it becomes clear that my sister is disabled.

The number is the word, and the word is knowledge.

One must be able to recognize power and grant freedom.

The old woman can't stand the strange girl.

She sits at the expensive, out-of-tune piano they've overloaded, in complete disrespect, with vases and fruit bowls, and pounds at the keys energetically with bent, but still strong fingers.

Mother and child play in the enormous nursery next door. The French doors are half open and the girl squats on the rug from the Caucasus, constantly peering into the next room.

She is absent, because she is deep within herself.

She winds locks of hair round her unusually long fingers.

Her gaze wanders. She knows everything.

The number and the question and the answer.

She will be free. The others won't.

The mother waves a colourful plastic car in the air before her daughter to draw the girl's abstracted gaze onto something tangible.

The child takes it unwillingly. She drives it a few times across the rug until the wheels get caught in the thick wool strands, and quickly loses interest.

A cheap substitute for real motion doesn't interest her.

She swings between the toy, which is foreign to her, and the tenuous adult conversation the two women begin again and again through the door and waves of music. The words seem strange to her. They don't mean anything, at least not what they seem to mean. She senses her mother's tension. She apprehends human emanations and cannot escape their clamminess. She can feel the suppressed anger like spikes. She knows it has to do with her. She is helpless. The old woman rolls her eyes. Then her mother loses her patience. Her violet-painted nails dig into her skin, through the material of her jumper.

I've just walked into the living room, intending to ask for money to go to the cinema, and I hear my mother softly threatening the child.

'If you don't behave, Splithead will come! I think I can smell him already.'

I roll my eyes. I don't believe in Splithead any more.

My sister looks at Laura, confused. She looks around.

She smiles and points to the ceiling.

Then bursts out laughing.

'He's up there,' she says in her peculiar singsong.

'Is there… has been there… There! There!'

Laura grabs the child's arm.

'Play! Now!'

'There... There... There!' she screams.

My eyes meet my grandmother's. She stands up suddenly; the red velvet stool in front of the piano wobbles. She shuts the lid dramatically. She stands still and is silent.

'Do something with the little one,' she says in a scolding undertone. 'Any kind of class – I don't know!'

Mother sobs audibly.

My sister says, 'Three.'

'And give her something to read.'

I close the door.

'Perhaps Dostoevsky.'

Finally my sister tentatively tries to express herself in Russian. My parents are delighted. Unfortunately, she can't understand anyone but us. The leap in communication was made in the wrong direction.

While I'm waiting with Laura and the child in a queue at the butcher's, she leans on the broad glass front of the meat display case.

The vendor snaps at her, 'Careful, glass!'

Terrified, my sister jumps back.

Glas means 'eye' in Russian.

She hides behind my mother's now-round hips and peers distrustfully at the blood-red goods spread out before her.

A pig's head sits between the steaks and the sausages, right at her eye level. It wears a suffering expression and a crown of radishes. Its legs are crossed before it like two swords.

She cannot articulate her fear. She freezes and can't be moved from the shop. Laura must remove her by force after finishing her purchases. My sister falls silent soon after this and doesn't say another word for a very long time.

With her conspicuously long skull, my sister lurches unsteadily from one piece of furniture to the next. How clumsy her movements look. She wanders aimlessly around the apartment, and the less she speaks with us, the more intensely she seems to make contact in other ways.

She sings; she coos; she has brilliant conversations with herself as long as she's alone. Her peculiar singsong stops abruptly as soon as anyone enters the room and her face hardens and closes. She looks up darkly until her glare chases whoever has walked in back out of the room.

The thing with the vacuum cleaner preys on my mind for a long time. I'm afraid that I have sucked everything human out of her.

'It's getting better,' my mother says bravely, and smiles when her friends ask about my sister. 'It's getting better. She likes to sing very much.'

'It will happen,' she says half a year later, utterly distressed. 'She is already talking a little.'

We're sitting at the tea table, beautifully set with the blue Russian porcelain. Between my mother, who now has a serious furrow in her forehead, and her colleague from work is a fragrant bouquet of flowers in a white vase.

'To herself,' I add, and am sent away with a painful pinch on my upper arm before I can grab a piece of cake.

When my sister turns three, my parents are finally ready to discuss her abnormality. My father has managed to dismiss all my mother's doubts for three years.

Three lost years. Like so many other practical and unpleasant things, the child's care falls to Laura. Without a word, my father hides away in his tiny, damp studio that cuts him off from everything like a firewall.

That is his secret world. Later, I will wander through its remains, amazed, a rediscoverer of Atlantis.

Without its inhabitant, it seems pointless and improper. I will find objects whose purpose is puzzling and messages from long-forgotten days. After carefully cleaning the dust and the dirt they become legible: 'Mischenka, I'm across the way having a coffee. Come in.'

Lev, who was so athletic, so happy to be out wandering in the woods, or through the flea market, or dancing at parties, can no longer move. He's getting a belly. In the morning, he downs coffee by the litre, just to get moving. The steady stream of visitors slows. The amusing Russian with his expressive blue eyes and violet-black circles underneath has changed his game plan. He wallows in the dark waters of depression.

Mute, with my mute sister on his lap.

All day long.

They sit motionless in front of the television on the worn

bentwood chair with a fur seat cover, watching random sports broadcasts.

Together they follow the monotonous repetition of the downhill slalom. I stand behind them, as I so often have, and can't bring myself to say a word. My eyes are glued to the back of his head, where his prematurely grey and now thinning hair reveals a small bald spot.

My father is no longer all-powerful.

In the evenings, my parents maintain a caustic silence. My mother throws him injured looks he is not able to counter.

Our hearts are growing ever more untidy.

Speechlessness takes over.

We are all tainted.

My mother's glassy beauty, which so often embarrassed me, has shattered. Earlier, she had been given noxious paints for a commissioned work and eventually develops an asthmatic condition.

We all turn against language; we all lose our breath. When there are no more acts, there are no more words.

We become mute.

I take out the old typewriter with its elaborate engraved mono-gram that had been stored on top of my wardrobe. It was the personal gift of a Prince zu Coburg und Gotha. It stands there, receptive, and unleashes a flood of memories: of sunny summer days and thundershowers that splash on my bare feet while I look for the flower-covered arcade of Grein Castle. I'm wearing a borrowed traditional, golden Austrian headdress that must not, under any circumstances, get wet and a silk sari that keeps slipping down and is too long. The owners of these pieces of clothing stand under the arcade and watch me with concern.

One is the art-loving owner of a large farm with a severe chignon. The other is a German woman with a second home in Calcutta. They both regret having saved my father from me, so that he could work on painting his stage set in peace. I have escaped from them and am staging my tribal dance in the castle yard.

Every summer my hunger for the stage reaches its high point in Grein. My father, always happy to make contacts, has joined a theatre group made up primarily of German artists who stage classical opera in the courtyard of the beautiful Grein Castle in Strundengau.

He designs the stage sets responsibly. Now and then he works with other set designers. Every year there is also an exhibition in the castle. It is my yearly opportunity to appear before the visitors, to play the errand girl backstage, to try on magnificent costumes and eat massive quantities of veal cutlets at the theatre group's expense and to spend three weeks being bored amid strange adults. Well after midnight, they can still be found celebrating at the long tavern tables, empty bottles piled high between guttering candles. I try to sleep on the narrow wooden bench in the back room, using my jacket as a pillow, under the sceptical eyes of waitresses in pink dirndls.

From the small observation deck behind the castle, you can see far out over the Danube and the surrounding landscape along the gently curving river. Down a winding path through the hillside garden, you come to the main door through the cool tunnel of the thick-walled entrance, past lanterns and tendrils hanging down almost to the ground and into the sun-warmed and rather inelegant inner courtyard. Still, the Virginia creeper that has overgrown the walls gives it a Jugendstil air. In the distance, you can hear the plashing of the fountain in the courtyard.

The Habsburg-yellow building towers up three-storeys beneath a shingle roof. The second floor is decorated with delicate arches and, between the columns, red-violet flowers pour out over the balustrades. In the centre of the courtyard reigns a round fountain, and to the side stands an ancient well with a peaked roof and a bucket on a rattling chain. Behind the castle, an unadorned basin is built into one of the walls. In it, an enormous, bearded catfish swims in nervous, twitching circles.

The catfish is the favourite pet of the lord of the castle, Prince zu Coburg und Gotha, who likes to be addressed as 'Your Highness' and who, let's say, has certain whims. The actors treat him with kid gloves. A single word from him can ruin the production. In support of the higher arts, he lets them use the courtyard without a contract or payment, but he also expects subservience in return. An argument with the director, who comes from Berlin and cannot grasp the old imperial habits, brought the project to the brink of disaster shortly before I arrived. The tension among all those involved is enormous.

Before we enter the castle the first time, the costume designer, a tall German woman with a big nose, holds me back by the arm.

The purple silk of her magnificent sari crackles as she bends down, fixing me with her beautiful green eyes, and asks me urgently to be courteous and well mannered with the prince. I'm keyed up with excitement, fidgety after the long car ride, but even more so from the news that a real prince lives in this castle!

This causes me some ambivalence. Russian literature is meant to abstain from any kind of positive depictions of princes or daughters of kings. Usually they're described as boring or malicious. They are colourless, the tragic result of shameless inbreeding, morally unstable and sickly.

Just as unpopular former members of government are simply airbrushed out of photographs, so particular figures disappear from classic children's literature and are replaced by others. The Bremen town musicians are a wandering commune of music-making animals, whose human leader convinces the daughter of the most prominent local bourgeois family to run off with him to the forest so they can continue to spread their agitprop. Puss-in-Boots is very popular and is printed in enormous editions because he is the first to trick the ruling class and outsmart the story's only intellectual.

I now know that I want to be a street urchin when I grow up. Because they're happy, healthy and content. I'm also not sure what I'm supposed to think of the castle owner.

I charge into the gleaming brightness of the inner courtyard and look around expectantly. A greying, moustached old gentleman in a beige suit is sitting at the fountain. Next to him, a polished wooden cane leans against the marble basin. The walking stick does have a beautifully carved knob, but there is no prince to be found. Disappointed, I amble up to the old man, call him 'Uncle' and ask where the toilet is. Behind me, the ensemble holds its breath like a huge, shapeless organism. The director has pulled a stained handkerchief out of his trouser pocket and is wiping his spotted brow. The old gentleman turns towards me very slowly and smiles.

He takes me by the hand. I resist at first, because I've been told not to go with strange men. My father follows him and so gives me the all-clear. He doesn't just show me the toilets, but takes me around the entire castle. We begin with the imprisoned catfish, who receives daily visits from His Highness. Panting, we climb the spiral staircase to the second floor. There, there is a museum of no interest to me. There are rocking horses from the Renaissance on which little princes once teetered towards their imaginary battles. They are covered with smoke-grey leather worn as smooth as silk and, against their gracefully bent necks, my dirty hands with fingernails bitten to the quick look especially rough.

From the walls, tall, elegant figures in suits of armour and hooped skirts look down disdainfully from their golden frames. I run screeching between the huge, dark oil paintings and the sluggishly whirling dust in the silence of the rooms. My words resound brokenly against the stone walls.

The director is short, ugly, manic and enthusiastic. His costume designer and co-producer is a tall caryatid with long, red hair down to her hips and a large nose. She is married to a tiny Indian surgeon. The troupe consists of musicians from all lands, a colourful mass of the most diverse characters. One time, the second violin runs off with the lead actor's wife the day after opening night. Another time, the director plans a concert evening, but suffers a nervous breakdown right before the performance, after several rows of seats were already filled with an expectant audience.

This year, they're presenting Glück's *The Reformed Drunkard*. The conspirators have concealed themselves with dark cloaks and my father's white masks. Lamenting, they sway across the stage, under a banner, meant to represent the sky. A chubby-cheeked angel with my features looks down on the stage with a furrowed brow, half hidden behind a baroque cloud. Heaven and hell lie one next to the other.

I'm wearing a discarded costume I found in the dressing room and am allowed to help sell tickets in the entrance to the courtyard. It is soon filled with an impressive mix of nobility, the prince's friends and relatives, and art lovers from the village of Grein. A few days later, there is a football match. As a member of the castle team, my father proudly plays goalie. We win.

I spend many lonely and tedious hours before opening night in the castle waiting for company, while the musicians tune their whining instruments, the singers practise, and the rest circle round the courtyard. I play in the gravel at the foot of the stage, but they soon chase me off since I'm in the way. They wreck the Barbie apartments I've spread out over the ground.

Then I pay a short visit to the fish in his simple basin. He is as idle as I am. I'm sitting listlessly on the broad flagstones, tossing the gravel, when the prince passes by. He sees me, turns and comes back after a short time with a large, unwieldy and heavy apparatus. I try to make out from a distance what could have been packed together in this bundle. A treasure chest? An old trunk? Piles of big books?

He carefully sets the package next to me on the bench. As the green case opens, I see the rounded silvery side of an old type-writer with his sovereign ancestor's name engraved on the front.

He rolls the first piece of paper onto the dusty roll and pushes the whole thing towards me. It now belongs to me. In an initial torrential wave of desire, I hug it tight in my arms. Then I'm overcome with reverence and I edge carefully away from it. We both remain silent, until he urges me expectantly towards the machine.

I hit the keys emphatically. I struggle with jamming keys and through my first work, *Eating Apricot Dumplings in Siberia* – a real page-turner.

8

Our family tries to recreate in Carinthia our beloved month-long stay in a dacha in the Soviet Union every summer. In Russia, of course, a stay of less than a month is not considered a holiday but a joke. Admittedly, we miss our little hut perched on chicken legs, a shack the real dacha owner used until the construction on his magnificent wooden building was finished. He then turned it over to us every summer. On the little cottage's warped veranda, my father often spread out before us the enormous collection of mushrooms he had just carried out of the forest in his worn rucksack. Porcini, orange poplar boletes, king boletes extra small to extra, extra large. He sorted them in mathematical spirals according to size on the sun-warmed boards. A dense, lush mushroom smell reached my nose as I gently stroked the velvet surface of their caps. At least we've found an Austrian Baba Yaga here.

We sought a refuge not far from Lake Wörther and found one. A partly run-down inn on the edge of a forest near two small, boggy ponds in a dark copse with soft water you can swim in as in warm ink. The inn is owned by an old, one-eyed woman. She has run the guesthouse here since her youth. She stands on the sun-drenched plateau of the inn's garden in the warm evening breeze, breathes the air in loudly through enormous nostrils, ringed with thick, grey fuzz, and thoughtfully tells my father that he can forget about his walk tomorrow because a storm is coming. My father looks up at the clear sky, at the softly rustling forest and again at her, with her dead right eye staring past him. He sighs and agrees. She has always been right.

Grandma Ada swims in the pond even when thunderstorms are approaching and rain is coming on. She has set herself so many lengths and she will do them. My mother runs agitatedly along the edge, sometimes keeping her sights on my sister, sometimes on the old woman. Mute with terror of the water, the child grips the bench for dear life, as if she had already suffered a shipwreck. Laura desperately gives them orders. Get out of the water! Get in the water!

The warm breath of the coming storm strokes the meadow. I'm lying among the flowers and grasses on my child's handkerchief. The meadow, dotted here and there with fruit trees, slopes down to the farmhouses and pastures below the village. Swarms of butterflies rise up now and then. The handkerchief is old. My thighs, now thicker, hardly fit on it any more. I look at all the movement between the blades of grass. An entire world. Brown and hard, juicy, green, soft and meaty stems with serrated leaves, with discreet flowers, with shiny fruit, inhabited by creatures harmless and biting, pretty and disgusting. I watch it all as my inexpert hand disappears into my shorts and the sultry heat of the afternoon grips my insides.

In the high grass to my left lies a worn pamphlet I stole from the inn's collection of dirty books and, hands trembling with lust and face red with shame, I smuggled it past the fat German in the next room, who, crestfallen, is now rummaging for it in the stack of magazines. He had told his wife he urgently needed to read up on the state of Austrian politics and now has wangled himself a free hour for nothing.

Heavily made-up naked young women writhe next to me in half-opened denim hot pants. I don't know if it's just their description that excites me – after all, they're not showing anything I don't have myself – or if it's the fact that I stole the pamphlet and am now lying on warm ground under an open sky, the rumbling on the horizon in my ear as I alternately leaf through them and myself.

Behind me, there's a path that leads to the woods behind the house. I listen intently for approaching voices or footsteps, but am distracted by the coming storm. Because I'm toiling fruitlessly, getting no nearer the goal, a balloon of rage grows inside me. From a distance, I can hear my parents coming down the path, with my sister cowering before the black wall of clouds and clinging nervously to my father's neck.

My mother coos.

She is tanned dark brown. She wears a colourful summer dress that compliments the colour of her skin. She tosses her long hair over her shoulder.

Rage springs right out of my core and over my hands like sparks on dry straw. Screaming, I tear the pamphlet to shreds. Little puzzle pieces with erect nipples and blue cloth scatter around me. I roll around on the grass among them cursing until something stings me.

In the meantime, the grown-ups have rocked the child to sleep. Her long, narrow head rests on the pillow in the crib and the adults sit on the bed across from her. Their voices are low and their movements cautious. The heat has them in its grip as well. They're afraid of being surprised by the other daughter or by the grandmother.

The rift between them is so great that their hands, working at each other's bodies, almost fail them. Now, now, now the deceptive intimacy could dissolve and leave nothing behind. They bravely keep at it, and for a short time they even succeed in closing their eyes and opening their legs and mouths.

Then I slowly sit up, my eyes narrowed to slits and my movements suddenly very calm. Pairs of butterflies still flutter ecstatically over the meadow in their mating dance. I stand up and target the copulating insects. I chase them until I can catch them and I crush the trembling little bodies to a paste or tear off their wings and destroy these too. I stand in a shower of drifting insect parts.

I gradually come round and, nauseated, shake the treacherous dust from my fingers. I look towards the woods, where the accusing eyes of animals seem to stare out at me, and burst into tears. I cannot undo the massacre.

Still standing, frozen, under the dark clouds, I see my mother run out of the house. Her hair and clothes are rumpled. She trips on the stairs, bangs her shin against a moss-covered cement step, but continues on quickly.

I feel such shame that I don't dare look at her for long as she limps towards me. I'm afraid she saw me and that my punishment will set in with the rain, a punishment that will wash me clean, a punishment I long for. I wince as she comes up to me, pushes me aside with her free hand and clambers up the steep path to the woods at full speed. The light cloth of her dress sticks to her shoulders. At the forest's edge, she turns suddenly and calls out to me that I should go back to the house; she has only hurt her toe.

The man stands at the window and looks out. He tries to see behind the curtain of rain, behind the foggy wall that has come between him and his wife. He curls one hand into a fist and holds his pounding skull with the other. It is empty, as empty as his hands that can neither offer tenderness nor accept it. He does not turn round when his elder enters the room. He takes a deep breath, to better hold his tongue.

Baba Yaga Girl

1

I STAND BEFORE MY FATHER; BETWEEN US IS HIS TIGHTLY-packed suitcase. I look searchingly into his face, into his remarkable light blue eyes expressively circled with rings of dark shadow. I reach my arms out to him in a sudden, strange impulse I myself don't understand. It's as if I were trying to enfold an insurmountable distance in order to reach him. In this moment I know that he won't come back, that I will never see him again. I despise myself for thinking this. I smile.

I push his suitcase out into the hallway. I push my feelings out behind it. I stubbornly announce that I don't want to go. My mother will take him to the train station alone. I had always stood on station platforms and watched as the train carriages rolled away until they were just dirty spots in the haze over the tracks, and was always a bit afraid of partings. This time, everything is different. I flaunt my new superiority: the strength of a woman who no longer needs her father and also isn't afraid to confront life alone. I insist that I'm completely calm. I dispense with our old ritual. I now have new ones. My good-looking boyfriend is waiting for me.

I slam the door. Like cracks in ice, I see hundreds of little furrows in its uneven, splintering coat of paint. I stare at them for a long time.

With trembling fingers, I redo my eye make-up.

My boyfriend's touch will bring relief.

Franz is probably more attached to my father than to me. He started a relationship with me to please his mother. I chase away the memory of how I lured him in. Franz comes from a nice middle-class family. His father holds an important position in a bank. Franz spends most of his time with his mother, who is a housewife. She likes to suffer. Franz would like to paint. It is obviously absurd to mention this desire in front of his father. Franz is quite talented, yet his pictures have something inhibited, hesitant about them. He is the kind of person who would rather not go the whole way, one who tries to sneak up by a side road.

I don't retreat.

I've been watching the handsome Franz for half a year.

How he calls forlornly for the teacher in painting class. How he arranges his hair with an elegant movement of his hand. How he always stands apart, neither with the girls nor the boys, as if he can't make up his mind.

His hesitancy decides for him.

He is my victim and will remain so.

When he doesn't respond to my advances, the next steps are inevitable.

I know about his fights with his father. I need a lure that is up to the mark.

Innocently, I invite the handsome Franz to our house. My father, Lev, the painter. My father, Lev, the teacher.

My father, the gaoler. But I am cleverer than Scheherazade. I know I can get around Father's jealousy by presenting him with someone who admires him even more than I do.

It works.

I've played for high stakes, just as I've learnt to do.

Together, the fish and the worm have wriggled off the hook. I will starve.

Later, I'm able to cultivate this hunger. There is pleasure in killing off one's cravings. If I'm going to be needy, then it is I who will decide when I will enjoy satisfaction.

I throw it all together in a bottomless pot: sexuality, drives, anxiety, it all simmers together, and I stir my cauldron like Baba Yaga. I am my own little hut on chicken legs that turns and turns whenever anyone calls.

The days up until the news breaks pass by randomly and un-exceptionally.

I take advantage of his absence and have sex for the first time in my room.

Franz leaves me strangely unmoved. The symbolism excited me more.

It is hot on this spring day, unusually hot. They haven't washed. They're sweating under the hastily spread blanket. A new smell wafts on the air, new material for the chronicler. The hangings over the bed are covered with murals: elves, fairies, the entire Grimm menagerie. On the wooden shelves are Dostoevsky and Tolkien.

The stuffed toys have only recently been thrown into a box. On her desk are opened books, drawing pads, a cosmetics box. Next to it is an opened pack of vaginal suppositories. Pushed in at the centre, they foam up out of the container. A pungent medicinal smell spreads throughout the room. She is embarrassed and laughs too loudly in order to mask the fizzing.

His fingers look like a girl's, long and delicate. She wishes hers were like that. With these fingers, he strokes her thighs indecisively.

She feels need rise up in her, but no arousal.

She wants to possess him.

She wants him to reach into her, into that part of her she has closed off. She hopes he will be able to reopen the door she is about to slam shut, that he will stick his foot in the door and stay. He should exorcise conventionality out of her. She closes her legs expectantly. He hesitates. He's not quite sure what he's looking for in her, in her body, wet with sweat, in her bed.

He catches himself thinking of her father, of his arms and his pleasantly sour smell. The bearded face superimposes itself on the girl's features, until he forces it away. Still, they bravely roll around in each other's arms.

He is awkward and fiercely resolute. His beautiful eyes flatter her. She fishes around for desire, but it eludes her. They have lit black Opium scented candles around the bed. The candles are cheap. They drip and leave strange spots on the parquet. The aroma lingers for days in her room and reminds her of her sin.

*

Then Jericho falls. The trumpet blast announcing the end of our world is a harmless telephone ring. Vague noises penetrate the dream layers. I just want to hide in my pillows, to flee. But the clamour in the hall spreads everywhere. I cannot escape it. Years later, I will still stumble to the telephone like a hounded lunatic whenever it rings at impossible hours.

My world is turned upside-down. When it stops spinning, I'm a half-orphan and I'm lying in my parents' bed, holding my dazed sister in my arms. We're re-enacting the father-mother dyad. She is confused by my sudden affection and unnerved by the commotion in the hall.

'What? What?' she repeats, sometimes softly, sometimes loud, because she is not getting an answer.

I look at her carefully. Her gaze, usually wandering without pause, has surprisingly stopped wavering and is fixed on me.

I should tell her the truth.

I say, '*Nada.*'

Suddenly she lunges at me, hitting and kicking, trying to scratch my face.

'Stop it, you idiot!'

'You're lying. You're lying. He says you're lying!'

'Who? Are you nuts?'

I deny him again. I hold her searching look. She pushes me away and runs out of the room.

'Where to?' I call after her, and watch the pillow beside me gradually regain its original shape.

'To him,' she yells back. 'To him.'

Then I hear her singsong in the living room, the monotonous aria of loneliness. I stay behind in the marriage bed.

The king is dead. Long live the king!

Still half asleep, they come out of their rooms. The girl has not removed her make-up. Her night-face has lasted until morning. The colours blend in the first little wrinkles around her eyes and give her features an air of indecency. The old woman holds her housedress closed over her sagging breasts with her claw-like hand and, in her haste, has left her dentures behind on her night table. The contents of the overturned cup drip onto her art books.

They stand around, incredulous, unable to decide what to do now that they have reached their goal.

The woman freezes with the telephone receiver in her hand and a childlike expression on her face. Her slender hand, on which she still wears her wedding ring, trembles but very lightly, like the string of a bow from which an arrow has just been shot. She waits to see what her body will do. She would like to throw down the receiver, stretch out on the ground, close her eyes.

That is the abyss they would like to let themselves fall into. They breathe in deeply and let the air out; it's almost like home.

The sisters disappear into the parents' bedroom. I let them go. The two women remain in the hallway between the living room and the kitchen door. It's all spinning like a wild carousel: rage, sorrow, hate, satisfaction, fear, relief. The wife hangs up thoughtfully. The connection between Russia and Austria goes silent. The breathing, the faltering, weeping voices in the background are gone. She slowly turns towards her mother.

*

My father is buried, according to his wishes, in Russia. He has squeezed himself into his mother's grave without asking our permission.

In Mother Russia's earthen arms. None of us could go to his funeral, just as before, none of us could pay our final respects to Baba Sara.

There is a leaden atmosphere in the house. The family is packed in cotton wool.

Just as I held my breath to remain silent in Mother's marriage bed, now I can't breathe in the hallway either. I don't want food. I don't want air.

I'm afraid to close my eyes in the dark. I lie awake all night as hunger, now just a strangely distant sensation, rages within me and melts away my protective layer. I leave the lights burning all night long and feverishly wait for morning, as if the soft strip of light along the horizon were medicine.

Here they are, finally: the admiring looks on the street, the envious looks from my mother. I don't care. Young men often call our house but can't make it past the hurdles my grandmother sets them over the telephone.

'Come home immediately, Mischka,' my mother hisses into the telephone.

The coiled umbilical cord is being stretched taut.

I snuggle into the worn, old-fashioned velvet sofa. Next to me, Franz has struck a pose and watches me apathetically through a cloud of marijuana smoke. He is busy with his grief work.

I softly answer, 'No.'

We are silent. I can hear her wheezing, even through the covered receiver, just as clearly as she must hear mine.

Franz snickers. He finds my daily phone calls with my mother and our agitation when we can't reach each other completely crazy. He goes home to his mother every Sunday and lets himself be spoiled. Then that's it with home sweet home for a while.

My friend Franz says, 'Come here, Baba Yaga Girl!' and reaches his hand out towards me. His smell is one of a new home. I close my eyes and let myself sink back.

The 'No' is the comb that, thrown behind the young heroine, turns into a mountain range. My eyes are veiled with smoke. The receiver slips from my hand.

In Russian fairy tales, there are figures who come to a sudden end because of their vulnerability or need for freedom. The old farmer and his wife have no children, so they satisfy their longing for progeny in an unusual way. They go out into a snow-covered field and there they build a girl out of snow. They return home exhausted. In the morning, the snow girl comes to life and joins them in their farmhouse.

The old couple are beside themselves with joy. They feed and care for the snow child, who helps them and brightens their lives. As long as it's winter, everything is fine. The child is cherished in the village and makes friends. But when spring comes with its first warm rays of sun, she wants to go and pick berries with the girls of the village and begins to melt. Reason and her parents' insistence triumph. The snow girl sits in the dark wooden house and watches the others sadly through the window. The old couple console her and remind her not to go outside before the end of summer. But one evening, there is a feast and the youth of the village all go to the dance. She can hear her friends calling her through the window. Twice she refuses. But the third time she can't stand being shut up in her room any longer. She follows the others and dances with them. The celebration is reaching its climax. A bonfire is lit. Girls and boys jump over the flames. The snow girl doesn't want to bow out. She jumps and disappears in a cloud of steam. No risk, no fun. Sometimes the old couple still see their ice child as a rainbow standing over their hut.

With loads of hairspray in my hair and an inhaler in my purse, I go to my first concert. I should have figured out beforehand what kind of act Einstürzende Neubauten would put on.

The crowd surges with excitement. I go down. The crowd is going crazy as I sink to the ground and stay there, surrounded by stamping, stomping and jumping feet in military boots and colourful tights, a nightmare forest of unpredictable movement. Dazed, I crawl through them to get out. Scared, I realize I'm struggling for breath. The way out is still a long way off. Sweat soaks my dress and makes it see-through. I can feel a draught of air coming from the entrance and am not used to having the skin of my thighs uncovered so shamelessly.

My fingers rummage through my purse, feeling for my inhaler.

It's gone. I'm a slut and don't deserve any better. My medicine is lost somewhere on the dance floor, and I don't dare go back.

Gasping, I lean on the damp wall and stare at the exit.

Franz has noticed my absence. The boy he was talking to so excitedly has probably disappeared onto the dance floor. He comes. He's looking for me. Mercifully, he catches me as I slowly slide down the wall. Waves of sound beat against my stomach as it vibrates to the bass, and they close over my head.

Inside, Blixa Bargeld is screaming.

Outside, I know I'm going to vomit right away.

My fear of suffocating is even greater.

I rest my forehead in Franz's hand and retch everything into the grass in front of the bar. The asthma attack lets up.

A dark and impartial summer sky hangs above us, cut with restless clouds. I turn my head towards it and laugh.

My mother can sense where this ship is heading and shuts her eyes before it hits the rocks. In tandem with my inner life, my clothing covers me in a black cocoon, artfully altered with scissors and trampled underfoot. Flying high before the fall. I want to shed my old skin, a mask under which my real face, more than just skin-deep, waits for me.

I set off into the world behind the looking glass.

I myself am the white rabbit. I follow the path into the dark hole and sometimes double back out of fear. Just as it did for Alice, the path goes straight down for a long time. Half of my head shaved, the other dyed; my throat, hands and thoughts dirty, I roam with impunity through the Viennese night. When I need to sleep, I'm not afraid to stay outside in the dark.

I'm asleep in one of the last underground trains. I fall asleep right in front of the enormous speaker in the U4 Discotheque. The noise crashes over me.

I sit on the steps to the dance floor. Movement stops in my eyes. I stare at the frenzied dancers as if I were a dybbuk waiting to enter them. I feel like I hold the strings in my hand as I shatter in the flashes of the strobe light, ready to reassemble myself again and again.

Sometimes people trip on me and fall over the railing.

Sometimes bodies wrapped around each other in desire bump against my feet.

A Madonna with platinum-blonde hair, ethereal in the neon light, stands at the bar. Our eyes never meet, and yet I've internalized her face. Her boyish body wrapped in lace, she reaches her tireless hands over the counter. I would conquer the world just to rise to her level for a day.

Time equalizes everything.

Twelve years later, our daughters are besotted with each other.

Above me, the black sides of the speaker are vibrating and the hairs on our arms and the backs of our necks are standing on end. The friend who destroyed our hair with bleach that morning lights her cigarette with a hand full of scratches. Her narrow wrist protrudes from her wide, fluttering sleeve. Even in the half-darkness, you can see the cigarette burns she gives herself every day. I watch this ritual, reminiscent of the skin decorations of African tribes, with wary ignorance. Her process is tedious. Mine has more precision.

My nomadic days are over. I settle down.

I come into my inheritance: my father's studio.

A hole in the wall on Margarethen Platz, in a little house with a wooden arcade, an inner courtyard covered in ivy and a leafy roof-garden Eden inhabited by a spry old Adam and Eve. Leaning on their walking sticks, they climb from their apartment window in slow motion out among bushes bearing flowers and berries. The city noises are swallowed up and no new noises are spit out. In the courtyard, all is unreal and quiet. In the courtyard stand an old lilac tree and time.

The toilet can only be reached through the overgrown access balcony. In autumn, the courtyard glows in strong shades of purple. In winter, sometimes the tea freezes in my cup. Occasionally, on a crisp winter's night, half asleep on my way to the toilet, I might stumble into a snowdrift with my bare feet or run into the neighbour, also on his way to the toilet and wearing only a T-shirt and his cowboy boots. Franz does not find my hysteria attractive and slips away more and more often.

I breathe in the smell of her loneliness.

She wants to seem tough and is troubled.

They sit there, under her portraits as a child of four, of six, of ten. She looks venomously at those she once was.

Her mother feels she and her world have been betrayed.

She presses her lips together and, behind her daughter's back, returns to the refrigerator the food her daughter had wanted to take with her. The traitor is treated with love; the one who is faithful reaps only reproaches.

The old woman slips the young one money in secret.

She wants to stop her granddaughter from leaving. She follows her to the door. On the doorstep, they argue about her blue-dyed hair.

'If you loved me, you'd leave your hair alone.'

'If you loved me, you wouldn't have a problem with it.'

Wild accusations are exchanged.

They scream; they cry.

Later, when the young woman is gone, the old woman will retreat to her room and scribble illegible declarations of love into her diary.

Mother and daughter anxiously cling to each other, wander through the empty rooms, buy furniture they can't use and cover every surface with plants.

The old one entrenches herself in St Stephen's Cathedral amid the observant Viennese. She kneels and is silent. She now lights three candles before leaving instead of her usual two. A quick glance back shows a flaming surface, a warm, breathing carpet.

Which father's daughter am I?

She is blinded.

The number must remain the same, for the number is the word, and the word is knowledge, and knowledge is power.

She narrows the eyes that have begun to fail her more and more often *until she sees the flickering red expanse behind the lids, where I, her Splithead, am waiting.*

She knows.

She tears her eyes open, stands up quickly and leaves before the high hall of the cathedral can reform around her.

She falters.

An alert tourist catches her.

The voices of the choir soar above her up to the ribbed Gothic vault, past the pictures of saints, over the crowd, and disperse in the dimness above the branching columns.

There will be no mourning.

They know how it works.

They cannot afford a separation.

In the living room, they create an altar of photographs and pictures of the dead one. Lenin, eternally alive in his mausoleum, now has competition in Vienna. Like two soldiers, they relieve each other on their silent patrols.

The man's clothing still hangs in the bedroom wardrobe, and his pillows and quilt are still on the marriage bed. His wife rolls fitfully at night onto his side of the bed until she bumps into the cool surface of the wall and wakes. Then she falls into a torpor.

Suddenly she is eight years old again, sitting under her brother's desk. She can hear her mother screaming in the hallway, and her brother bends down, half frightened, half gloating, and tells her that her father has just died in the hospital. It wasn't his father. And once again, she wasn't there. All men sneak away without saying goodbye. She pulls her knees up to her chin, hugs them to her chest and succumbs to silent, hysterical weeping.

The old woman is content: everything is going as predicted.

At night, the shadow of fear she spreads to her daughter reaches to her. Then she tosses back twice her usual dose of sleeping pills, to which she has long been addicted.

During the day, she beguiles her daughter.

'That's how it is with men. Didn't I tell you? They die right out of your arms, leaving nothing but cold. And if they don't die on their own, we hound them into the grave. That's just how it is.'

The quiet child becomes even quieter. She is frightened by the silent faces that look down at her from the walls. Her eyes closed, she feels around the corner for the light switch. She forces herself to go in. She is brave.

She knows I am here.

Then she sits in their old chair in front of the television without turning it on, sucks her thumb and counts to three. Her mother chases her away with hysterical screams when she catches the child there.

Franz, the fickle traitor, discovers a passion for ethnology. Painting reminds him too much of my father. He suffers much more from his loss than he's willing to admit. He's disoriented. He resents my lack of lightheartedness.

I'm no longer the magician's daughter.

I'm an heir without a throne.

The studio brings up difficult questions. He avoids it.

We meet now mostly in clubs since his parents don't allow his friends to visit. I despise him for this, but I can't afford to let him go. I'm like someone who can't swim clinging to a wooden plank full of rusty nails.

The studio is full of my father's materials. Piles of dusty paper, bits of clay, colours, rotting, stinking colours, warped shelving filled with all the odds and ends he'd picked up to work with later.

From the one barred window, you can catch a glimpse of a corner of the roof and a slice of blue sky. When it rains, it's like being in a run-down barn. I lie on my dusty mattress on the dirty floor, my clothes piled next to me, and watch the water as it falls. The world is bathed in restless silence. There is no sound aside from the steady patter; there is only the room, me and the rain.

Out over the wooden walkway, out to the street, out of my own skin, out of my mind. But I can't escape myself.

I start travelling. I avoid staying away for more than two weeks. After the fifth day of every trip, I develop a fear of loss that makes every holiday hell. Travelling companions resent me for it. I am the bane of every happy tour group. Even worse are flights. The anxiety of being at the mercy of another's whims is trumped only by my fear of heart-lung machines.

Feeling like a complete Judas, I sell my father's enormous printing press that took up the centre of the room. With a friend of my mother's, I get rid of a vast amount of paper, cardboard, books, scraps of cloth, old newspapers. The matriarchy has triumphed.

2

THE IRON CURTAIN HAS FALLEN. THINGS ARE HAPPENING
in Berlin. Franz and I take off. Prague races towards us with every
clack of the rails under the train. Darkness is falling. Lights flicker
on and flash by. I press my forehead to the damp window that
frames the starry sky and push the warp-speed button. The space-
ship shudders.

We tumble onto the square in front of the main train station
very late at night. I've barely set foot again onto Eastern Bloc soil
for the first time when I feel a blow in the pit of my stomach as if
I'd stepped in front of a wrecking ball. Somewhere between the
Castle District and the Charles Bridge, I fall to my knees.

It's warm, a clear summer night.

Meanwhile, Franz is musing out loud about the advantages of
Prague's rent-boy scene. The urge to grab him by the throat and
throttle him grows even stronger. He is driftwood on the flood of my
past. I want to go to a hotel. I don't have enough money with me.

'I bloody well want to enjoy myself,' he hisses at me.

'So do I,' I scream back, 'but I have to be able to afford it.'

That hits the mark and he shakes me off. The Prague night closes in on me. The next train to Berlin leaves at dawn. Franz will stay for a week in a nice hotel and will go to fancy nightclubs. He will assuage his loneliness with shopping orgies and then with the pleasant company of a sales clerk in the Yamamoto Boutique. He'll call my mother's house a few times to ask after me, but won't reach her. What luck! Out of worry, she probably would have cancelled the trip to America she'd just booked.

Then Franz heads home. A four-person sleeping car, whole hog. I've put off my trip home. I'm still searching.

Laura couldn't care less about the communal apartment in St Petersburg. But that is what I'm looking for. My new digs are in a half-ruined house in East Berlin. I'm one of the squatters who have taken it over.

I lie to Laura. I tell her I'm staying with a friend.

'What happened with Franz?' she asks directly.

'He's daft,' I end the conversation.

'But cute,' I hear her say as she hangs up the phone.

I live among all kinds of people thrown together: proletarians, students, petty criminals, alcoholics, idealists. Communal kitchen, communal building, occupied bathrooms. In the midst of it all dogs roam, big ones, little ones, mutts. There are also radical feminists living in the building. I twirl my red lace bra over my head and earn a slap. The underage train-station whore, with pimples and a big chest, takes my side. In her room, there is nothing that even remotely reminds me of Aunt Musja's plastic boudoir. A broken mirror, a flag with a skull and crossbones, a potted plant. No-one knows where she came from and no-one listens to her.

The Filipino has jade-green hair and a fresh shiner round his left eye. In the evenings, he offers me tea. We squeeze onto his old sofa. Franz's bed is as soft as down and always freshly made. The Filipino is softer than I am. Exhausted, I fall asleep next to him. He covers me with his jacket.

Some have eaten sausage samples at the supermarket and catch glandular fever, which can also come from eating cat meat. There are festivals all over Berlin. You can sit on a former rod of the Iron Curtain, swinging your legs and belting out songs. The streaming together of East and West has just begun. Embracing and a sense of optimism. Still. I balance on the edge of a piece of the Wall and am stranded with an English puppeteer.

Franz waits for me in Vienna. I have a guilty conscience and call my mother. She sounds very far away.

'When are you coming back then, Mischka? Franz calls me constantly.'

I sniff contemptuously. 'Wimp,' I say.

'He always wants to talk about your father,' she says.

I flirt all day. Later, I call Franz.

'Tell me it's not my fault,' I wail.

What I've never yet said to anyone slips easily over my lips moist with snot. 'I miss you so much.'

'Come home, Baba Yaga Girl. I'll send you money for the sleeper train. Just come home.'

My misstep leaves him strangely cold. The Filipino and I burn through half of the money and all I can afford to book is a seat. We hang out in front of the Memorial Church. Punks, beggars and jewellery vendors nest on the sun-warmed steps. They're all cadging. If Franz saw me here, he'd disown me.

I've scarcely arrived in Vienna before my mother decides to take off. On short notice, she packs up my sister and Grandma Ada and disappears, headed towards America and our relatives there.

They pack their bags. They know they'll return; still the trip makes them very anxious. The woman examines the old one's suitcases and throws out half of what she's packed.

'We don't need that much ballast, Mother.'

The old woman needs the weight to anchor herself to the ground. She begins to panic. They fight over the backpack.

Meanwhile, the little girl sits on the sofa, in nice new patent-leather shoes. She sees my face and hers mirrored in the tops of her shoes and chews on the strap of her bag.

They are not expected. They will fly anyway.

The little one is used to being sent to relatives whom she's never seen. The old woman is hoping that, in New York, she will finally be able to hold her son in her arms and explain away all the misunderstandings.

They drive to the airport without speaking. The old woman sent a letter that morning. It's meant to arrive at the given address before them. They check their bags and watch them disappear into darkness on the conveyor belt and treat themselves to a meal in the cafe from whose window you can watch the aeroplanes land and take off.

The old woman seems calm.

The number is the word, and the word is knowledge, and knowledge is power. Her heart is racing under her sporty blouse. She has woven the straps of her child's backpack round her fingers. A cat who tries to perch on too high a branch is difficult to rescue.

The woman tries out the role of ringleader, spins on her axis to catch a glimpse of herself from the side. Her daughter on her arm, her eye on her mother.

Then a long, heavy sleep. Below them the ocean, above it dark sky. A journey together across the darkness, catered by Do & Co.

In New York, it's windy. Full of hope, the old woman searches for familiar faces in the crowd that forms a colourful wall behind the barrier in the arrivals hall. She doesn't see well. The crowd is still unrecognizable.

She listens intently. She tries to pick out the one, the right voice from the sea of people. She's reluctant to leave the arrivals area. There's no call, no waving hand, even after her daughter pulls her over to one of the yellow taxis and makes her get in.

The taxi ploughs through the city's canyons that look nothing like the boulevards of St Petersburg or Vienna's narrow streets. Glass chasms filled with light and movement. They look forlornly out of the window and hold each other's hands. The child is asleep with all the fingers of her right hand in her mouth.

The driver frowns at the address. Red-brick buildings with fire escapes. The suitcases are heavy. Streets with numbers instead of names, fitting for her mathematician son. The two women hope he will be home when they arrive.

*

The taxi stops. The driver puts their bags on the street next to the whining girl. The car drives away.

They look around. One door looks like another.

The woman is hesitant to ring. The old woman begins a litany of sorrows.

One of the black doors opens. A round, dark-skinned face appears, surrounded by small, woven plaits.

The old woman shrinks back. Hippies, even here!

The young man smiles. Who are they waiting for?

For the Russians? They're at the airport. Their relatives are flying in today.

The woman sits on her suitcase and starts to cry. He comes up to them. His voice is melodic, but they can hardly understand him. He brings their suitcases into his apartment, escorts the old one, the girl and the woman inside.

The two watch their belongings warily.

'They'll be back soon, the Russians,' he reassures them.

He sets out some tea. He has seen his Russian neighbours make it often enough: dark tea is brewed and served with lots of sugar cubes and sipped out of small glass cups in silver holders.

Conscious of their figures, the ladies decline the sugar and sniff at their cups. Drugs?

His apartment is small. The windows, behind colourful curtains, are closed. Reddish light filters in.

He smells of spices and fresh popcorn.

He asks for the Russians' telephone number and calls them. The mathematician's answering machine fills the room with bad English. The neighbour tells him his relatives have arrived.

They wait.

It is evening. They sit around the glass table. The television is on in the next room. The ballerina is doing her exercise routine in front of it. Lively music penetrates the closed door and breaks on the silence that hangs over the table. There is sushi and salad. Diet Coke and bottled water stand on the table. No-one drinks alcohol here. The mathematician's wife smiles.

For more than half an hour they have thoroughly discussed how they managed to miss each other at the airport.

The neo-New Yorker is still smiling. She brings out the photo album she keeps on hand behind the table and proudly shows them the accomplishments of her son, who has become an architect. Here a blue-print, there a model, the silhouette of a thin, mirrored glass tower he had co-designed. Even the New York sun shines in the pictures. Humbled, the woman squints against this family's radiance.

The young architect is away at a conference. They don't expect him until morning. The old woman is beaming. Her son is still hiding from her, but still, he hugged her, placed a fleeting kiss on her flaccid cheek, and now he's sitting with her at a table.

He sips nervously at his water glass. He hasn't eaten a bite. He watches as the women who have gathered in the living room push the food around their plates with mannered gestures.

His daughter doesn't join in the show.

She is always the winner.

He would like to sit with his daughter and watch her precise movements. He glances at the door of his small office. The cost of showing his mother he's successful is high. He has to work late into the night just to keep his position at the university as an exotic and unimportant assistant. With iron discipline he will talk about his career advancement in the next few days – if he even opens his mouth at all, that is. The old woman will tiptoe into his room and find him bent over his desk. She will gently lay her hand on his thin shoulders, and before she can take in the warmth of her child's body, he will abruptly pull away from her.

The sister watches her brother, too. She looks for his face as a child beneath his beard and wrinkles. The hardness around his mouth fades, the longer she looks at him. They're back in their children's room. His desk towers above her, massive and heavy. He rests his big feet next to her on an embroidered pillow. He has taken off his slippers.

She chews on her plaits. She is nervous. There is the sound of voices outside in the hallway. He sits there motionless. She thinks he's doing his homework. For three long years of pre-school she has dreamt of also being able to do such important work at her own desk: to sweep the hair from her forehead, to leaf through books, to fill page after page with strange signs until her fingers are covered with ink, in her own, respected field of knowledge that only she is allowed to touch. Later, their mother will come in the room and, with a serious expression, put on her glasses and thumb through the pages, nodding thoughtfully. And she would get a feeling of accomplishment.

*

157

Her brother gently wags his feet in their sweaty socks. There is stitching on the heel. Their senile great-grandmother, who lives on the living-room sofa, sewed it up. She no longer knows anyone's name and can't remember much of anything else, but she occasionally recites, unprompted, ballads, darns socks and embroiders flower patterns on the bedspread she made from her husband's army coat.

It's good she doesn't know anything.

She would be incensed by her daughter's lie.

She has been lying for years.

Israil. Not Igor.

There is no time for her mother any more, no history.

I could betray her.

But I am devoted and loyal.

On the surface everything is smooth. She would like to climb out and look around, like the Little Mermaid. She crawls out between her brother's legs. Then she notices that he's not writing and he's not reading, either. The books have been carelessly thrown down next to him.

His face is buried in his hands. She stands up and leans against his back. She can feel his warmth through the jumper. He sighs and relaxes a little. His back arches against her carefully. The leaves of the trees rustle softly in the courtyard. The smell of petrol wafts in from the street.

The noise of scattering gravel. A car drives up outside; the doors are jerked open; the alarm goes off. Then brief, but emphatic swearing. The alarm stops. Doors slam. Steps in the courtyard. Both children smile.

Then her father calls her, 'Come here, my little dove, come!'

*

Their mother's second husband is an enthusiastic amateur handyman who fits out his cars with security devices and accessories. He spends weeks developing them, then leaves most of them uninstalled.

He has just walked into the apartment. She hears the deep voice with which he opens the New Year's celebration every year as Jack Frost, hidden behind a mysterious curtain. 'Where's my girl?'

The boy starts, shakes off his daze and pushes his half-sister aside. She beams, prances and shoots out through the door. As she buries herself against her father's thin chest, she notices that his face is tense; his cheekbones jut out even more prominently from beneath his beard than before. She looks up at him from below, with a smile that is anything but childlike. She knows this look will make him melt, like the ice girl in the fairy tale. She winds her plaits round his throat and presses up against him, breathes in his smell and feels herself protected by an impenetrable shield, under a secure dome that spreads over her invulnerably.

3

'JUST GO OUT, MISCHKA,' FRANZ SAYS.

I collapse on the sofa, which engulfs me in gold-coloured velvet. 'Go ahead.'

He is the dark side of the moon. He's inaccessible, and yet all I'd need to do is stretch out my hand. He is my little golden fish who has granted me a wish, then disappeared right away and for ever into the deep water.

I let my head hang, while Franz, in a good mood, shifts the mouse attached to his computer by a tangled cable, just as I'm attached to him by the umbilical cord of my unborn child.

The time to cut the connection is over. Now it's official.

Parents are informed, an apartment found, a wedding date chosen, without caresses.

Franz dutifully sees to furnishing the nursery over the Internet. He whistles through his teeth and orders a grey silk shirt as well. I clear my throat.

He doesn't turn round. He's done enough for today and I've seen enough.

'Go out, if you want, Mischka,' he says again. 'You could get yourself some shoes for the party first. We do want to look good.'

I smile.

'You've got the money.'

I don't move from the sofa. We wait.

Finally he turns his handsome face towards me and hands me two notes. He looks for signs of elation. I don't even try to pretend for him. I take the money without thanking him. He frowns and goes back to his virtual store. I say nothing and listen to the noise of his fingers on the keyboard. At some point, he admits defeat.

'Just go,' he says again. 'You don't have to come back before tomorrow morning. Or tomorrow midday.'

I stroke my round belly.

The tears are strangely foreign. I can feel them rise as if from a cool reservoir, as if I were a caretaker accepting or handing them out as needed.

He shakes his head. He has given what he could. Even if I were to stay obstinately rooted to the spot and refuse to speak to him, he couldn't give any more. Finally I get up, put on make-up and leave the apartment to spend his money on useless things, then demand more two days later. I know what I'll get, too, regardless of how much I'd like to have. I descend on the temples of fashion and, in a few seconds, go through the money I've earned with my suffering. I want the lustre of the names on the labels to shine out through me. In my carelessness, I throw the masterpiece in the washer and, after a few cycles, I find it again as a little girl's dress. I drain Franz dry and he lets me starve.

We speak the same language but can't understand a word.

I'm a master of translation, but fail before I start. A wide river lies before me, its water turgid and bile yellow, barely crossable. I set out. I'm no longer afraid.

After countless separations and rapprochements, I have finally married Franz the indecisive. The marriage hasn't exactly brought us closer, but it hasn't pulled us apart. He wants men but needs a wife. He needs me as a front for the world. I need him as a front for myself. And so we have the perfect relationship.

Happy mothers rejoice over their unborn children. I feel weighed down. There is no way back. The aeroplane has taken off and we're flying to Lithuania. This is how it was when I brought home in a basket a cat I'd been given.

My womb gives a lurch. I don't understand what it's doing; it's incomprehensible. Then my heart does the same and, as other body parts follow, I finally catch on that my child's birth has begun.

The lover, who has appeared at the breakfast table, is given a roll with butter and thrown out.

'I'm busy,' I announce to his bleary face, and hand him something to drink. He waves the steaming coffee cup, uncomprehending. I quickly close the door, before he can say my name.

I look out of the window and watch the bulky figure of the man I'd just ushered out of my apartment as he chews his roll and disappears round the corner. He seems to have left the coffee cup somewhere. I breathe out.

I still have to pack a bag for the hospital and go to my physio-therapy session. As the cramping wraps a net round my body, I whistle to myself, casually open the small chest and search through the arsenal of pyjamas. I choose a pair of tiny leggings and knit jackets. I still can't picture how they will look filled in.

I call Franz and set up a meeting place and go to physiotherapy. The therapist has a beard that reaches down to his little paunch. We sit quietly facing each other on our mats like two Buddhas.

I don't listen to him.

My senses are turned inward. Outside, it's the others.

For the first time, I experience the child in me as an independent being that wants something and can set it in motion. We know there's a lot of work ahead of us that we can best accomplish as a team. This movement is a dance, like a flirtation in which two people move closer together and then apart, more and more emphatically, until there is pain and self-abandonment. This ecstasy will not deceive me.

At night, when the contractions are more rhythmic, I force Franz to come to the hospital with me. He doesn't believe a thing I say. Fine then, we'll do a trial run.

We've been dozing for more than two hours already in the spacious bed of the alternative birthing centre. The midwife has said goodbye again. There is nothing to do yet.

Around midnight, I wake up. My child's skull is hitting my pelvic bone. I can still hear the impact five years later. I can't breathe. My bones are cracking. My hips are suddenly ten centimetres wider.

Like Moses striking water from a rock, water gushes from me and floods the bed. Franz wakes and takes off running to find the staff. I feel around for my pocket mirror. I sit in my blood on the birthing centre's linens.

Push, push, push.

Then the doctor hands Franz my child. I sit there, the severed umbilical cord between my spread thighs, where the midwife kneels. I must telephone. The cosmonauts are expecting an update. The midwife frowns, her forehead as sweaty as mine. Now and again she tugs impatiently on the umbilical cord still hanging out of me. We are waiting for the overdue afterbirth. I demand the telephone once again. The nurses are piqued. Still, it's a private hospital and well paid by my husband. I am heard.

As I listen impatiently to the tones through the receiver, Franz wraps my daughter in silk, hugs her to his chest and rocks her in his arms. Franz with the face of a Madonna. He takes on the role of mother. He is more than motherly. His is a truly inspired motherliness. Holy.

I must first share the news of my daughter in order to comprehend it, to feel it. The world is fragile. Only what I express exists.

In the beginning was the word. There was no love outside of our gazes. My daughter's gaze wanders over my face. I feel her cool, perfectly formed fingers. She grabs mine decisively. Her nails are long and well rounded, as if she's just had a quick manicure.

I am quickly sutured up. So thoroughly that my attempts to shit over the next few days fail miserably. The slit is closed, but it's already too late. I've seen the circling stardust, the motes of dust. I've felt the dizzying pull sucking at me. I know the place.

I have started dreaming in Russian. I can feel the unwieldy language pile up in my mouth like driftwood. I feel unruly emotions building barricades between me and my Viennese garden plot. The old me awakens. Her hibernation is over. My clothes have grown too tight for her, so has her cave. Fragments fall on me like a shower of gold, like the contents of a chamber pot. Step right up and win!

I am waiting for something I can't name, and I feel how its absence makes me furious. I loathe the pretty Russian girls who cross my paths jabbering and wearing too much make-up. I loathe the fat gentlemen with gold watches who want to throw their money at the girls. But I also loathe the cultured ones I meet around the museums.

For more than fifteen years I've avoided Russia, ignored it. And now it stands before me, gaping stupidly, and I can't find the words. The fear that I could disappear, like a stone in water, has gone.

I can't sleep at night. I stand, bending over my child, hardly daring to breathe and listening for omens of disaster. I close the heavy curtains, because the sunshine makes me nervous. The midwife watches me with concern, but she's 'alternative' and doesn't tolerate meddling.

*

I sit, important and fat, in the centre of the event and listen to stupid pronouncements on pregnancy, birth and motherhood. I reluctantly nurse my child, who's soon switched to bottle-feeding, and feel oddly absent, as if, at the moment of delivery, I'd also left myself behind in the world, like some stock culture that has successfully divided into cells and ceased to exist.

I inadvertently keep my diary in the refrigerator and develop a fear of eating beef.

4

The number is the word, and the word is knowledge.
Which father's daughter?

Sooner or later every escape comes to an end. She has ridden the horses into the ground, gone without food or water and given everything she had to get away. She knows the journey is ending. She can't be bothered with travelling companions who can't keep up. She knows lonely treks through the mountains.

She knows ascents.

She thinks of the steep mountain paths around Alma Ata, dusty and hot. The apple-tree branches, weighed down to the ground under the marvellous red burden. The scent of the ripe fruit.

The mountain air, piercingly fresh, and loneliness make her feel she could fly. The leather straps of her heavy backpack cut into her shoulders, but she forces herself to go on. She breathes deeply and calmly. She knows her strengths. She starts to compose her will, short and very modest. The art nouveau wardrobe to her daughter. What else is there? A massive, archaic bracelet with inset stones she had bought in a mountain village in the Caucasus. Cushioned on old velvet in the

167

wooden box. Whoever wears it has magical powers.

Her last will, distributing her possessions, is ready.

The jewellery is her trophy. Her favourite granddaughter will inherit it. It is worthy of a real princess. She shall fearlessly continue the journey led by the jewellery's coarsely stained stars.

From the top of a skyscraper, I look tensely out over the window rail. The air in the room is stuffy and full of medicinal smells that make me dizzy. I press my nose in the crack of the tilted window. The roofs of Vienna, pierced here and there by Gothic church spires. A sunset, a loosely scattered flock of black birds. They soar up along pre-determined paths and sink down to the spot from which they stream into the city, an enormous double helix that constantly revolves round itself and remains still. I look away, towards the sun. When I'm no longer blinded and can make things out again, the pastel-grey space above the city is empty, as if the birds had never existed.

I am newly divorced. I left my child with my mother, who's too worn out by excessive despair to help Ada. I'd like to call her, but don't have any mobile-phone reception.

I'm waiting for Grandma to come back from testing. I sit on her bed in the small hospital room and spend the time waiting for her in conversation with the patient in the next bed.

Time passes as in a sporting event. With Ada's transplant I watch as time catches up with me, runs next to me, neck and neck, then disappears into the distance ahead of me to the sound of the spectators' applause. I give time the trophy.

Trapped in the small room, we look searchingly out into the Viennese night at illuminated apartment buildings and trains passing over the arches of the elevated track. The beams of the headlights, the loud droning of the nightclubs, the hospital cafeteria, even the scraggly bushes down in the courtyard, they are all separated from us only by a pane of glass and yet are part of another world to which we have no access.

Ada's condition is bad. She struggles for breath. She will live because another has died. Another's chest has been opened for what she needs.

I can feel her envy and am ashamed of my fear. A doctor soon enters the room. The stranger's heart is too strange. Death and money bring people quickly to the point. She thanks him calmly, waits until he has quickly closed the duck-shit-green door behind, then turns to the window and is silent. I wait for my grandmother.

She still has lipstick on her lips. She smiles as she sprays herself with rust-red Betadine in the shower at the Vienna General Hospital. A red half-moon in the steam. She fixes her hair. The bitter smell reaches her nose.

She thinks of a child's scraped knee and tears. She thinks of a leaning barn, a half-opened door, of stiffened bodies to her right and left. She hears distant laughter. She hears her heart beating as loud as it did then.

She feels a breath blow past he; like a magnetic field, her hairs are drawn in the direction it is blowing. The laughter grows faint and disappears, and it is once again quiet within her. She breathes in deeply and softly out.

Israil disappears. Igor is left.

She cannot weep. She sees the rust-coloured trickles run down her shoulder and knows she is alone. Her feet in the brown shower tray.

The door opens and my grandmother is pushed in on a wheelchair. Her immobility is disconcerting. Small and delicate, she sits there with a blanket spread over her knees. I see her face, pale and composed.

I want to hug her but she moves away and, instead of her hand, gives me her silver-grey leather bag.

'Go downstairs and get me a coffee, Mischenka.'

'Are you sure–' I begin, but she interrupts me with a gracious smile.

'Or anything else. You'll find something.'

I sniffle.

'Go now,' she cuts me off. 'Please.'

I can still touch her uncut body. She and I are both still whole. She has politely closed herself off from me. The door slams behind me. I run down the hallway to the lift.

Ada's bag dangles from my arm.

The buffet is shut. I'll have to find the vending machines.

I dig through her purse. Something clinks and I grab for it.

It's a locket attached to her house key. When I open it, I see myself, wearing a black felt cap and with blue streaks in my hair. It all goes downhill from there.

When I try to put the medallion back, the purse spills open from my shoulder. Ada's passport falls open on the floor. I bend

down and pick it up. I look at the picture and the name underneath. I have to look twice to believe it: the name is Rahel
Israilowna.

5

WHAT DO YOU DO WHEN THE WALLS CLOSE IN AROUND YOU?
What do you do when the hand you've held as long as you can
remember and since you learnt to speak squeezes your fingers in
a clammy grip so tight you have to prise them free? For her, time
stands still, but for you, it's still running.

Under the cheerful yellow sheets my grandmother's child-sized
body lies curled up on its side. She appears very focused. Her gaze,
wide open but hazy, passes over my face to the trees in the hospital
gardens, bending in the wind.

I lean on the empty bed next to hers.

She has nothing to say to me.

'Go.'

Yet she is the one who is leaving.

'Who is Rahel?' I'd like to ask. But I don't have the courage any
more.

There is no room for contradiction in her affection and love is
a pearl that is not often thrown before swine.

I put the steaming cup of coffee on her night table and rearrange the bouquet I've brought. I don't dare touch her, as if overstepping that boundary would slow her down. I close the door behind me.

She closes her eyes and searches.

Her wrinkled fingers feel the surface of the canvas.

She pauses. What she's searching for is very close.

When she stops searching, she will find it. She fights against old shadows that come to her at night in ever shorter intervals. She needs strength to hold back the pictures that crowd around her. The reverberations of a fear and the echo of the fear of fear.

Israil. No, Igor.

The battle renders her mute and blind.

Her head begins to swing back and forth, like mine. She senses the shadow and rises up against him.

Igor. Igor. Igor.

The opaque gas-like layers alternate with clear bands of memory.

Igor. Not Israil.

Isolated pictures rise from the fog.

Which father's daughter am I?

Figures, voices, the number is the word, and the word is knowledge, and knowledge is power.

Outlines of cities seen from a great distance, grainy pictures of faces.

Israil. No, Igor.

My surface melts into her inner life, grows louder. The number is the word becomes more demanding, and the word is knowledge becomes three-dimensional, and knowledge is power grows all-encompassing.

I am the number.

Israil. Not Igor.

Israil. Israil. Israil.

As all-encompassing as my gaze.

The number must remain the same.

The number is three and we have arrived.

Three is the word.

Three is knowledge.

Three is the power.

Three dead.

Three marriages.

Three daughters.

Three mothers.

Three husbands.

First married at seventeen, divorced at nineteen. Inexperienced. Full of suffering. The second love, just before the war, with a patriarchal man from the Caucasus, with whom she has her son. Escape from St Petersburg, besieged soon after his birth. Barely survived the famine, with her small son travelling across Russia on a freighter. Rural life in her second husband's homeland. The end of combat is also the end of her second marriage. She won't let anyone hold her back. Her career advances. She is appointed to the university and leaves her raving, macho husband, who breaks off all contact with his son. She returns with her child and, not long after, enters into her third and last marriage.

From this marriage comes her daughter, the much-desired late child, pursued by her half-brother's dark and baleful looks. The third husband soon falls seriously ill. The illness carries him off after a short time and he leaves behind a widow turned hard as stone and the terrified girl, now defenceless against her brother's spitefulness.

She will not save her daughter.

This, too, has been promised me.

She looks at me and drinks in the pictures that I generously offer her. Faces, landscapes, passages from her books. There is room for everything and in the continuous motion everything has its truth.

Everywhere a hue and cry, as her small son plays with his little wooden horse surrounded by their belongings on the ship's deck. She knows she has saved her son. She is calm. She has no reason to be anxious because I am with her. She has promised me her first child in exchange for my help and I have agreed. The vault is full of fake gold I have spun. Soon she will be married for the second time.

Her first husband's laugh, the young good-for-nothing who charmed her despite all his flaws. The boat trip with him and his secret love. Having forgotten her jacket at home in the rush, she is freezing in the cold wind. She stares at the crinkled surface of the lake, over which the first reddish leaves are blowing.

She is calm.

The more experienced rival offers her her coat as he rows.

Her own games as a child in the well-kept city apartment they moved into after the war. Her mother's benevolent gaze, the damask curtains, soft rugs that swallow the noise and porcelain toys. The kitten she was given when she was five years old and the waves of joy she could barely stand when she caressed the soft body.

Her face, childishly round, with flax-blonde hair and a fringe. Holding her mother's hand in the evening light. They stand in front of the barn, in the dark outline of the door, looking straight down to the left.

She knows what they both see.

Her fingers let go of the cool linen and are raised towards me. Fear can be inherited.

The widened eyes of the child, crouching between motionless parents in the hay, are fixed on the boards of the hayrick. Shafts of evening light shine through the gaps in the wood and are repeatedly broken by the marching bodies outside. It smells of dried grass.

It is deathly quiet inside. She hears the heavy breathing coming from her own throat and mixing with that of the grown-ups. She knows her mother is praying soundlessly in Yiddish. She can feel the words breathed onto the back of her neck, but doesn't dare take her eyes from the slightly opened door, through which she can hear snatches of conversation. The stamping of soldiers' boots, the squelching mud. Just when it sounds like they are leaving, the tumult returns. Her mother's grip around her chest tightens, her hand over the tiny young heart, whose rapid pulse beats against the mother's fingertips. Screams. Laughter. The timeless silence is torn like the thick cobwebs across the hay barn door as it is thrown open.

Hulking black shapes against the night sky.

Her mother screams.

Her father is silent. Sweat runs down his forehead.

176

They storm in, many of them, out of control, raging, a spring tide stinking of alcohol. The father throws his arms up, windmill and Don Quixote in one. In a flash, they are on him and throw him aside. Her mother is still praying.

A loud crack.

The mother's lamentations are drowned out by the girl's piercing screams. She grabs her mother's neck and holds on with such a death grip the men cannot separate the two.

'Make her shut up!'

'She'd better shut her mouth! And come outside.'

The woman nods her head, but the child, following blind instinct, redoubles her efforts and digs her fingers even deeper into her mother's warm flesh. She is holding on for her life. She is savagely determined.

'Enough,' says the second soldier. 'Leave the Jew women. Come.' He turns and disappears into the fog. The first soldier still wavers undecided between the miserable pietà and the door. The mother's chin has sunk onto her chest and a thread of saliva hangs down from it.

The child is still bawling.

Through the crack in the door she can see the glare of burning buildings. Outside, round the corner, a body lies in a black pool of filth. The father's forehead is still damp. The boot print next to him slowly fills with water.

The child stands and stares at him. She thinks she can hear a sound so high-pitched it is almost deafening. Her scream has taken on a life of its own. It has returned.

She feels a bursting inside. A splintering. A crumbling.

She is falling into thousands of fragments. She stands in a shower of

177

particles. *There is an undertow, a centre of gravitation, a coming together, a collecting. She silently acquiesces. She is wrapped in a warm, protective cover. The colours of her surroundings fade; the landscape around her pales, but only slightly, as if a sheet of Plexiglas had been placed between her and the world and has dampened all the noise outside. She holds her breath and gives herself over to this weightlessness I have promised her for eternity.*

I keep my promises.
Everything will remain the same.
No more pain. No fear. No life.
Idling instead of moving.

The mother, saved by the child, is now hated by her – no, held in utter contempt. She reads; she learns; she steels her body with merciless exercise routines morning and evening. She will hound away the memories that occasionally surface inside her with pain and sweat, just as she was once hounded.

More than anything she wants equanimity, peace, control.
She will stop at nothing to get them.
She wants a cold heart.
For that, she needs me.
I have cut her off from fear and from life.
The price of that brief moment of powerlessness in the hay barn was too high. She has never forgiven her mother, the only witness, for her origins and the deadly flaw.
Now she is no longer alone.
I, her Splithead, will follow her, will take away her pain, her joy

178

and her desire, and will grow bigger and bigger. My hunger grows with me.

She will hand her children over to me.

I am faithful. I can take everything.

She believes this experience has hardened her against fear of any kind. Whoever forgets he was once a victim can easily become a perpetrator. Whoever refuses to look pays.

First just with sleeplessness, then with increasing blindness. Yet she still does as she pleases.

She changes the name of the father who betrayed her from Israil to Igor. She calls herself Ada, not Rahel.

She hangs a cross round her neck.

She is blue-eyed and blonde. She doesn't stand out.

Ada Igorovna. The future professor.

Her mother, however, carries the seeds of the fog within her. It will be years before she sinks into gluey oblivion. In a late revenge, she won't recognize her daughter. Lying under the beautifully embroidered blanket. It's just as well. The less she knows, the more I know.

The next morning, she has advanced quite a bit further. Morphine has proven a good provision for her journey. It makes her steps calm and certain.

I am a sprinter and can catch up over short distances and keep my promise. I will run beside her for a while yet, long enough for us to speak still, as is recommended.

Her bed is cut off from the window with a sheet. Behind it sits an older woman who doesn't dare to pass by our ritual and escape into the hall. So she is forced to watch the shadowplay.

My mother and I have set up postcards of Grandmother's favourite icons around her, the archangel on the swivelling table, the Madonna and child on the trapeze bar hanging over her bed. They leave me cold. I read Tibetan mantras. Building blocks of religion that can be expanded upon at will to create fantastical buildings with onion-domed towers, Escherian archways and dark dungeons. Now and again I compulsively look in the mirror, to check my make-up.

Her eyes are closed. She doesn't need deceptive light to find her way. Her sightless face with dilated nostrils swings searchingly back and forth as if she could scent the way. I don't need to hold her gaze to keep contact with her. The path is narrow. We jostle each other now and then. We squeeze together.

My mother stays behind.

I no longer notice her.

Ada's once muscular, now thin arms swing out forcefully as if she were climbing a steep slope with a stick, as if she were reaching out, trying to grab something. An uphill climb. Ragged breaths. Every now and again we take a breather. Then I leaf through *The Tibetan Book of Living and Dying*, looking for directions.

Time begins to flow at different rates for each of us. I understand that I will have to jump off soon.

Everything is so clear and simple that it confuses me.

Three times we prepare to jump.

Three times we draw back.

I feel the draught of air, the sensation of being pulled upwards, the loosening of all ties, the pan shot of the camera slanting off to the side. Then over and past me, leaving me stranded on the plateau, for a time as motionless as she. I cautiously lay my hands on her stomach, which is still pleasantly warm. Dripping with sweat, I've barely had a chance to catch my breath when a muffled groan escapes her chest, no longer shaken by any heartbeat, as if she were still undecided. The sound rises up and hangs above us as we stand clutching each other. The woman in the next bed jumps and bolts out into the hallway.

6

SHE SITS AT HER DRESSING TABLE, HER HAND ON THE *threadbare silk of the book in front of her. There are no Cyrillic letters on the covers, no onionskin dividing the pages.*

Her wedding ring is still on her widow's finger. She gave her husband's ring to their daughter. It fits her daughter's thicker finger perfectly. For her part, the daughter has taken off her own wedding ring and put on her father's. She is finally married to the one for whom she was destined from the beginning.

She once again carries her father's name and wears his ring.

The mother sits in front of the curved mirror. She doesn't waste a glance at her face, with its contours beginning to blur. She strokes the smooth book cover, as if she could once again touch her mother's face, or her husband's skin, or her own skin as a young girl. Outside, darkness is falling slowly, the light is refracted, and it's only just possible to read. The letters dissolve into the twilight, the blue-tinged light. The letters become peculiar and strange, like the years that have passed. She narrows her eyes. Fine lines etch themselves in her face. She lifts the book higher.

'My love for her is painful!' it says there in unsteady script. Odd. She writes 'painful' as if it were a forbidden love affair.

The woman shakes her head.

Her mother's diary trembles in her hands. The writing dances before her eyes.

'My love for her is painful because I am afraid of losing everything,' she deciphers further.

'Whenever the child crosses the threshold of the apartment, I suffer. What can I do to stop her? I can't hold on to anything, and nothing holds on to me. I can no longer forbid her from doing anything.'

'The child,' she writes, as if it were hers!

But everything did belong to her, everything, everything.

The first child, the second child.

Even the son-in-law.

The whole family.

She puts the book down abruptly on the glass top. She slams it shut. Dust flies up. For pages and pages, just the granddaughter. The granddaughter. The granddaughter.

And before that: the mathematician. Both stories of loss, both treasured because absent. And what about her? And what about her, who faithfully stayed by her side, through all the years? She hears her insides rumbling violently. She feels nauseous.

At least her lost daughter has returned.

She has left the hostile world. She has finally accepted it, dutifully put on her helmet and turned on the microphone. It's difficult to breathe in the atmosphere of her homeland planet. Now, when it's too late to comfort the old woman.

Now the family is back the way it should be: mother, daughter, granddaughter.

Until the next man comes onstage, sooner or later.

Then the game can start again from the beginning.

No-one leaves the space that I determine.

The number must remain constant, for the number is the word, and the word is knowledge, and knowledge is power. There can be no changes: the lesson has been well learned, swallowed with the mother's milk and set in the marrow.

I see to that.

Adas become Rahels, mothers become widows, and widows become new, self-confident women. Rebels turn into housewives. But I didn't want to play the lottery.

So that I won't constantly lose my face, I look into my pocket mirror. Occasionally up to thirty times a day. Everywhere and always, I look into the mirror. Yet I'm always haunted by the sense that, behind it, I can recognize another pair of eyes looking at me with calm concentration.

I hate the way my face gapes at me out of pictures in the family photo album and out of many portraits by my parents. A ridiculous mask that makes me unrecognizable. I look in the mirror of my lovers' eyes; I look in the newspapers; I look for myself in artworks in the museums, in pictures of my relatives, in glassy surfaces in bars. What a shame I can't perceive the lover or the artworks, my family or the bar, even though I don't find myself in them.

I sit at my mother's dressing table in secret when she goes to meetings at the special school or when she goes with her Russian friends to Café Diglas for *Apfelstrudel* and coffee.

She seems to be discovering the night. I smile like a wise, embittered old witch. I know the night and its supposed secrets. They don't tempt me any more. When it gets dark or the lights go on in some unknown area, she slips out into the night. I hand her shield and sword, tell her politely if her lipstick is right and lock up the heavy castle as the heels of her pumps clearly sound her way down and out.

Soon she is going out in the evening more often than I, who have had enough of men and candlelight. When I can no longer stand sitting in front of the television, I roam through the silent apartment, in which both our children are asleep. I look for a long time at the black spots on the floor of the small room that used to be mine and is now my sister's. I believe I can still clearly smell the scent of the candles. This chases me back to the studio, to where my folding bed, covered with the blanket made from the military greatcoat, stands next to my child's crib. A half an hour later, another tour of the past accompanied by countless glances in the mirrors. I end up at the dressing table, staring into the eyes of my mirror face. I want my walking hut back, the hut that listens to my every word! My own four walls, surrounded by a pretty little fence made from human bones.

It's getting dark. The sofa in my mother's studio is already made up. My daughter is asleep in her crib.

'The hand towel! Do you have it?'

No. I don't want to wash.

'Mischka! The hand towel!' her voice insists.

Dirt is dangerous.

Dirt hides beauty.

What is true is seldom beautiful.

But I would like to feel like an antique vase that has been freed from the dirt. I want to be found.

For the time being I must be patient, until I have my own apartment.

My own personality. My own life.

I settle down in half a house, and a rustling suddenly showers down around me. Nudes of my ex's new alibi-bride, for which my mother is responsible, rain down around me from the shelf. The mood is downright autumnal. The pages fall as if from far away.

Beige brushstrokes everywhere, crossed by small, black triangles of hair. The subject reclines upon the same sofa on which I am now supposed to dream my sweet dreams. Mother arranged her in suggestive poses on a red velvet throw. With pleasure, she neglected to say the slightest word about it to me. For years after our divorce she kept inviting Franz to tea. With his new wife. I sit there like Danae in the divine golden shower that heralds no danger.

It's hard to fathom what such harmless things as weddings can do to people. Incredulous, I hold the gold-rimmed invitation in my unlucky hand. I have to read it twice before I understand that the handsome Franz obviously wants to find out one more time, even though he doesn't want to acknowledge a thing. My handsome ex Franz meets me in the supermarket between the paper towels and the cleaning supplies. There is a suspicious gleam from his finger. Asked about the ring, he hands me the invitation.

I will obey this invitation. Amid strangers and old acquaintances, this is my second wedding dance, in a flowing blue dress and with blood from an abortion between my legs. Filled with spite, I've ended this pregnancy.

'But, Mischka, you know perfectly well, in what kind of situation … I mean, really,' he said.

I took my pocket mirror out and looked in it carefully. Then I snapped it shut.

'Now think about it. Please just think about it for once.'

No-one came with me, as they had before to the birthing centre.

In most cases, you enter the House of Death alone.

I show up, bleeding, at his wedding one week later. Without a date.

I should have looked for the toilet much sooner.

But I am grimly determined to last for one more dance. I move under the cover of the dimmed lights.

Enough is never enough. The world is large: in the next room you can eat your way around the globe. Sweet adzuki-bean paste in light green and pink, fresh from Japan, and decorated with elegant dabs of soy sauce right next to the golden Habsburg-yellow fried Wienerschnitzel on a silvery tray, mozzarella with cherry tomatoes and basil in the Italian colours, spanakopita with tzatsiki, Polish apple tart with big pieces of apples in their own juice, spicy and strangely foreign-smelling Nigerian stew with a large, crudely carved serving spoon, and blini with caviar next to a bowl of salted sour cream. Anyone not on the dance floor can be found lingering between the two long tables, temporarily covered with linen tablecloths, paper plates and plastic tableware, and circled by hawk-like glances.

Fruit salad towers colourfully in an enormous cut-glass bowl, topped by a huge pineapple. As a five-year-old, I would have offered my life in exchange. The table next to it is overflowing with bouquets and wreaths.

The African father-in-law successfully attempts to fill his son and my child with grilled chicken. My ex-husband's sister watches him attentively, wrapping a curl round her finger and resting her face, which looks so much like my daughter's, idly on the palm of her hand. A red silk scarf is draped round her pale throat. She looks severe, and a little lost. A Japanese couple has grabbed front-row seats. She has long bleached-blonde hair and a miniskirt; he is greying and stern. They present their son like a performing monkey. On his father's barked commands, he takes up various fighting postures. A delicate, girlish face, intense focus, trembling thighs. In two years, his father will choke his wife half to death as the son films him on his mobile phone. Mother and son will flee the family apartment carrying only a small suitcase.

The crowd claps. Some are disgusted.

I look discreetly into my pocket mirror, with my weepy, panda-bear eyes.

The music starts up again. A male East Indian dance troupe in suits and ties hop around like Pan and cock their heads simultaneously. Their leader has gelled Johnny Depp hair and a sparkling Swarovski crystal death's head on his collar.

Everything is spinning – the couples and the lone wolves.

My daughter sways, smiling blissfully, happy in the crowd. Occasionally we rub shoulders when the stream of dancers pushes us together.

Her step is sure. I take credit for that, too, and I'm proud of it. I gave her the gift of firm ground beneath her feet, roots that wouldn't sprout for me. My past bleeds out of me. Where I was at home yesterday will be different tomorrow and gone the day after that. It doesn't bother me any more.

My first child turned out well. I denied myself the second. My current lover is married and intends to stay married.

I'd like to kill the handsome Franz, like the unborn child last week. A Baba Yaga can do that. In fact, one expects it of her.

The music swallows all noise.

I breathe deeply and dive in.

I'd wanted to be a mermaid, but only ended up as a Baba Yaga.

I'd wanted to be a mermaid, with flowing seaweed hair and eloquent eyes.

I wanted to lure men to my rocks and would have been better off having to stay mute and dance on painful feet to get a human soul.

Around me are whirling Indians, Japanese, Turks, Viennese, Africans, Germans. If I have to choose between two stools, I'll take the bed of nails.

7

As the two families fall apart, the relatives get back in touch. The Iron Curtain has recently fallen. The emigrants still don't recognize its similarities to Salome's veil. People are trickling through the gaps to the West, hungry, frightened and full of hope.

Those who stayed together in clans pity those who have lost so much. Those who have lived in Europe for a long time feel sorry for those now leaving for Israel, just as they once felt sorry for the stragglers who went to America and turned their backs on the old continent. There are stumbling blocks enough, here as well as there. The newly Americanized feel sorry for those who have never set foot in the land of unlimited opportunity, for those who didn't have the courage to adopt the American way of life. Those who live in Israel scorn those too cowardly to come to their true homeland.

None of them understand those who stayed in Russia. They smile at them as they would at an old watchdog, who is finally unchained but still seeks refuge in his doghouse.

Unlike the first wave of emigrants, the second generation is a bit more informed. Rumours spread. Myths and tales of success arise. The well-educated have real opportunities. Uncle Salomon, the plumber with the broken nose, is carried along on the stream of the highly qualified and ends up with his family in Tel Aviv the following year. Ljuba and her daughters will settle in Jerusalem. Unaccustomed to the heat, they are all soon reduced to figures that look just like mine. I'm sent pictures that show them on the beach in risqué bikinis, pictures of the three of them in new clothing eating exotic fruit, beaming with pride. The only one who stays is Nathanael, who wrested his kingdom from his older brother and has no intention of jeopardizing it.

However, before it has come to that, the first generation of emigrants still eyes their old homeland. They hurry; they want to see everything in the country as it was when they left, to recover the past and consolidate their advantages.

I feel like I must go there, even though the idea repels me. Something inside me has decided it's time to see my father's grave.

To go through the dilapidated Jewish section of the graveyard, to kneel down by the headstone and look thoughtfully at the inscription, just as I've seen them do in soap operas. Perhaps even then place a bouquet on the grave, as warm tears run down my face with its tragic expression, and depart with faltering steps, supported by an elegant companion. Ideally, I would have a parasol and a veil to protect my faultless pale skin. I know it will not go like that. It doesn't matter. It has to happen and I'll take it on. Now that I've found an apartment I'll move into soon, I'm hoping to stop my craving for mirrors by going through the looking glass of my childhood.

With a queasy feeling, I pass through the gangway's plastic tube into the uterus of the enormous jumbo jet. What I can see of twilit landscape through the small round windows is covered in gloom.

Before the plane has even taken off, Vienna falls away behind me.

A sense of muffled horror gives me tunnel vision and I take my seat. I will spend the next three hours sitting there drenched in sweat. Strangely, there are only four other passengers in the huge aeroplane. They're sitting a few rows back and stare at me suspiciously. Plump, motionless apparatchiks in grey, motionless suits. Standardized looks, standardized faces. Briefcases at their sides like weapons. Stiff white collars, bulging double chins, intelligent piggy eyes. Their eyes roam over my hair, my greenish face, the black dress, the funny little bells I braided into my hair so I wouldn't get lost, my gnawed fingernails, the Indian rings, the huge earphones that protect me. They can't make any sense of me.

At this point, only the old Soviet officials who have permission to work in the West fly on the ancient Aeroflot aircraft. Their idea of Viennese businesspeople whom the USSR sporadically sought out after the early, tentative opening does not correspond to my appearance. No-one else boards the plane. After half an hour, the aircraft sets off.

Two stewardesses appear in the Kafkaesque emptiness of the passenger hold, almost lost in the dim light. I feel the pressure of the increasing speed on my body as if I were being pushed through the seat. The wheels leave the ground with a jerk. I close my eyes and only open them again much later, when the night has already closed in around us.

The flight attendant puts a plastic tray in front of me. On it, she has placed a colourless piece of chicken garnished with grapes and a slice of bread. After a horrified look, I recognize the same menu of thirteen years earlier on the flight to Vienna and I gag on the meal. The tray starts to tip. It slips out of my hands and the chicken lands on my lap. Before I pass out, I clutch it for support.

I see a small, old-fashioned bottle. The stewardess waves it under my nose as, terrified, she encourages me to smell it. I want to get off. Right now.

I only realize an hour later, when I step onto Russian soil, that I'm still holding the chicken leg in my hand. The officials are so taken aback by my appearance that this detail doesn't strike them as particularly odd. Disgusted, they rifle through my Indian back-pack. I proudly show them my identity. My passport picture shows me at the height of my punk flowering, with a silver chicken leg in my ear, my hair and eyebrows royal blue, like my bug-infested cap. My rabbit is also in the picture; his head, pressed up against mine, fits perfectly under my chin. The Russian customs officer, hoping for a bribe, demands that I show him the animal. Enough joking around. With a shudder, I remember my stupid face, the crying fit, the idiotic scrambling through my cosmetics bag until I can pay him off with used lipstick. My tears, and especially my empty bag, convince him.

A stamp is hammered onto my passport, right next to stamps from the GDR, the USA and Israel. I'm international livestock with valid papers. Live freight. The bang jolts me from my trance. I get rid of the chicken and look in vain for a Coke, that new homeland's welcome.

I don't know where I am. I snap my tattered passport shut, stuff it in my backpack, stagger towards the frosted-glass door of the arrivals hall. I look at my spiky boots with buckles. I hope my relatives find me frightening; at least then the trip will have been worth it. I spent weeks putting together a daring outfit.

The frosted-glass door slides open. I recognize a pudgy older woman with glasses, leaning forward expectantly. Aside from me, there's no-one else to pick up. I approach her hesitantly. This is supposed to be my pretty aunt Alla? The funny redhead in a miniskirt who read me fairy tales? Her face shines with joy. She calls my name. Mischka. I have arrived.

As we leave the building to go to the bus-stop, I can feel the earth squishing and all of its intolerable weight sticking to the soles of my shoes. I fight the panic rising in me and yank my feet high off the ground, wrenching them away from Mother Russia.

In the bus to St Petersburg, we stand on guard surrounded by countless people. The bus is overcrowded; its back end keeps scraping the ground and sending showers of sparks over the asphalt. My entrance into the city of my birth is clouded by an old woman nagging rhythmically behind us. I only realize once we've pushed our way out onto the street that she wasn't scolding randomly, but has been laying into me. After a few steps, she has me caught, unexpectedly and inescapably, in a rising flood of accusations. I stand there, my mouth open. Beside herself with indignation, she screams at me to leave the city this minute. Russia doesn't need people like me. It's a disgrace! Auntie reacts calmly, but aggressively, scaring her off with just as much eloquence and enjoying every minute of it.

She pulls me after her into the underground. We take the deep escalator, illuminated by magnificent chandeliers shedding light on drab, pallid hair, clothes and faces. The walls are lined with marble. People turn to look at me. Some smile; some laugh at me. One greets me as the little bluebird of happiness. I decide to get my knitted hat from my backpack. My aunt is delighted. She has a topic of conversation for the next few weeks.

We've barely sat down in the carriage when she pulls a plastic bag from her purse and presses it into my hands. I open it and recognize strange black stumps with a pulpy mass oozing out of cracks in the sides. Bananas? Yes, three-week-old bananas. She'd searched them out and kept them safe until my arrival, without allowing herself to enjoy even one of them. I feel guilty, so guilty that I claim the excess while she takes for granted that she will share what little is left. Guilty, because for all my fears, this country still amuses me and I can leave at any time. I choke down half an antiquated banana.

We don't say anything until the final stop. We pass the once splendid but now decrepit Winter Palace, which, from its size alone, is still impressive, as are the daunting wrought-iron lanterns in front. Instead of stately teams of horses before the entrance gates, there are just small figures of people on the wide steps with umbrellas opened against the biting wind.

Through the winding alleys with canals and arched bridges like Venice, past cosy little wooden snack stands, some with completely bare shelves but filled with customers, others lavishly stocked with all kinds of delicacies but without a single customer. As I head purposefully towards one of the shops, my aunt holds me back, laughing. This one is just for the 'more equal' citizens. We don't have any *valuta*, special vouchers. They're reserved for Party bigwigs. The Western kid promises to be hugely entertaining.

Later, on the difficult hunt for presents for my daughter, I wander around a giant *Univermag*, a kind of shopping mall, located in the historic arcades of the city centre. A huge stuffed bear used to stand in front of it back when I was little. This is where Uncle Vanja squandered his pension every month, in the off-licences.

I'd like to bring her a piece of jewellery, like the one my grandmother left me. My crown princess should get a small token from the lost kingdom. The glittering glass cases of the jewellery department are impressively outfitted with plush, midnight-blue velvet. The rooms are large and crystal chandeliers hang from high ceilings. The saleswomen are overdressed and sullen.

I bend over the counter full of expectation and recoil: the velvet display is completely empty.

The sight is disconcerting. I look, uncomprehending, at the face of the gold-framed clock suited to such a high-end shop. It says four thirty in the afternoon. I turn to the saleswoman, who has been watching my movements with interest. They must have put everything away already, I suggest. The woman bursts into infernal laughter that makes her beehive hairdo shake. Everything here was put away long ago.

On the breezy banks of the Neva, which smell like the sea, the golden spire of the Admiralty still bores into the dull sky. The wind whips up foam-capped waves on the surface of the water, which stretches endlessly from one bank to the other. The steps down to the blue-grey water are covered with greenish slime, out of which rise bronze griffins. Wings obediently folded onto their backs and gleaming brass fangs bared, they're ready for anything. One on either side of the stairs, they stare fixedly and hold each other hypnotically in check. Like Sinbad, I would offer them a big chunk of my thigh if they would only take me straight home.

The boulevards, flooded with traffic, are unusually wide. The dimensions of the old city are so grand that Vienna, in comparison, seems like a dinky little model of a city. I cower before the mansions. The view appears distorted, as if I've taken LSD. A bright yellow trolley bus bends ponderously round the corner, its long feelers extended delicately in our direction.

Aunt Ljuba's apartment, where I'm meant to sleep, is a symphony in brown plastic. This material, openhearted and self-revealing even from a distance, has been modelled in wood grain for sake of decorum. Mimicry. A rustling beige plastic bead curtain dangles in the entrance. They treat all natural finishes with care. The

197

colourfully printed tablecloth in the kitchen is made of PVC. The one in the living room probably isn't, but they've covered it with a thick, see-through layer of polyethylene, as they have the sofa. Certain is certain. The smell hits me, drags me nose-first into my childhood like a badly trained dog.

The hallway is bursting at the seams. Everyone has come to welcome me. They laugh, hug me tightly, smother me with kisses, treat me informally, as if I had spent the last years going in and out of this apartment and were here today to celebrate a birthday. I don't recognize most of the faces that are joyfully pressing in on me. Bearded and clean-shaven, wrinkled and smooth, covered with lotion and make-up, with glasses and without. They don't introduce themselves because they assume I know them all. They soak me in their smells and in their stories. I feel dizzy. I'm ashamed of the slight sense of disgust growing in me.

I can't share their enthusiasm. Love goes in through the stomach and out through the anus. The family-amoeba has me trapped in its centre. They give me pictures of my grandmother Sara, whom I look so much like, and they feel justified by this resemblance in treating me like her. They're all screaming at once. Like Baba Mascha, like Baba Yaga. Then they reproach me for dishonouring Baba Sara's memory with my impossible hairdo.

My twin cousins, still fat, are a massive and steady anchor in the surge of the extended family. They extract me from the crowd. We slip into the side room, while Ljuba, Galya and the other women set the enormous table, laughing and yelling. In no time flat, the table is overflowing, just like the fairy tale. Then the twins fall on my suitcases like 'The Cudgel in the Sack' and marvel at the Viennese wonders.

They don't fit in the clothes I've brought with me. I've waited so long to spread my Western life before them, generous but superior! Just for once, to savour the taste of victory. My sacrifice has paid off. They haven't been cut to the quick, but they have been able to see their horrid world as one wretched whole. I disdain them for this. And for the poison brewing inside me, I disdain myself as well. They have snub-noses and gorgeous manes of hair. They have lots of colourful rings on their squarish fingers, with which they rummage through my T-shirts more briskly than the customs officers. Beautiful, sad cow eyes and dark fuzz on their upper lips.

The solicitous housewives have baked all day for me. The kitchen smells of things I can only remember preverbally. They treat me with a mixture of awe, joy, pity and greed. Uncle Salomon's daughter is pencil-thin and would be very attractive if it weren't for the huge glasses that hide her face behind cheaply framed lenses. They don't have contact lenses here. She's quite vain. She confesses that she sometimes goes out without her glasses. Then she depends on her sense of touch to get by. The tone of our interactions is that of the sober exchanging of goods. I never answered a single letter they'd sent me.

In the living room, they've prepared countless presents for me, which adds to the birthday atmosphere. The men open bottles of wine and sit in the living room smoking their pipes and philosophizing. I avoid the couch with its bright, embroidered cushions. I know my father drew his last breath there, his head on the lap of my fattest aunt.

They're playing Vyssotsky, singing one of my father's favourite songs, 'Capricious Horses'.

They sway to the music, lost in thought. I think of my daughter waiting for me in Vienna, lose the rhythm of the music and serve myself from the lovingly prepared buffet.

The feast for my arrival is costing me dear. On my request, my aunt has baked the cream-filled meringues I loved as a child but can't get in Vienna. I devour them, shovel them in and stuff myself so full I can't move. After the party, I sink down on the flowered sofa and fall into a deep sleep. I spend the night asleep in my clothing, still wearing make-up, on my father's death bed, and I wake in the morning with sharp pains in my abdomen. I become hysterical.

This is the punishment for all my sins. I'm going to die here and now. I close my eyes and lower my head back down on the armrest as if a guillotine basket were right underneath it. My submission lasts five minutes. Then I remember my daughter, jump up and storm, weeping, into my prudish aunt Ljuba's bedroom.

She bolts up, terrified, and runs to the phone in her tent-sized beige underwear to call an ambulance.

I writhe on the sofa. The pain lessens somewhat, but the drama increases. I'm convinced that I'll never be able to leave this country again. The doctor arrives. He kneels down next to my sickbed, frowns over his gold-rimmed glasses, opens his old leather bag, which smells strongly of medication, and pulls out a huge glass syringe. The last time I saw one of these was in a Vienna museum. I am suddenly healed, before he can put me in an unspeakably embarrassing situation. I'm told to put my fists under my 'bare buttocks'. He's using a medical expression that every Russian knows, but I don't.

'My what where?' I whimper.

'Surely you know what "*jagoditza*" means. Stop with the act,' his voice rises impatiently. Worse cases are waiting for him out there than this spontaneous fit of hysteria.

My mind is racing. *Jagoditza* sounds suspiciously like *jagodka*, which means 'little berry'. I sense that there is little time left before he completely loses patience. He raises the huge glass syringe dangerously close to my face.

I try to fend off his help and ask again what it means. To my relief, he lowers the implement and looks at me with a mixture of indignation and concern. Then he repeats, very clearly and calmly, 'Your hands. Under your left *jagoditza*.'

I blink helplessly and don't move.

He starts yelling. I start bawling.

My pale aunt opens the glass door and waves my Austrian passport in front of his face. For the next half-hour, he grills me about Greenpeace and the Green Party in Vienna without treating me. I'm happy I evaded the weapons-grade injector and fear has cured all pain.

With my aunt singing his praises, the doctor finally goes off to save whales and leaves me behind with a diagnosis of 'hopeless

overeating, gastritis'. I fall back asleep and don't get up again until
darkness falls.

'Quiet,' Ljuba says.

She pants as she climbs the last few steps. I stand, oddly trans-
fixed, in front of the green varnished door with the same scuffed
nameplate that used to be half a metre above my head. Her en-
couragement is completely unnecessary. I don't even dare breathe
too loudly, so that those inside the apartment won't hear me. I can't
leave the shadow realm, no matter how hard I try. I'm the one
holding myself stupidly back. I'm still falling for the old trick and
I turn round. I'm chilled to the bone from the cold, damp wind
that accompanied us from the cemetery. Neither my jacket, my
scarf or my skin can withstand it. I'm still holding Ljuba's umbrella
in my hand, like Mary Poppins, waiting for the wind to turn.

'So ring, then!'

Her perfume reaches me before her words, heavy and warm, a
smell that has enveloped me ever since we left her brown plastic
apartment. I'm certain that I'm permeated with it and will smell
it long after I've returned to Vienna just as I did on the bus ride,
the long stretch on foot to the cemetery and all the way to my
father's grave.

As we approach the Jewish section of the graveyard, my steps
slow and become lighter. My feet scrape the grave. Beautiful old
headstones, some completely covered with vegetation, jut from the
ground like dragon's teeth. It's foggy, as so often in St Petersburg
at this time of year. The swans are somewhere. I can hear their

cries through the fog. Before, I fed them in the nearby park with Ada while she told me about 'Swan Lake'. The poor black swan was unlucky compared to the others and got no food from me as punishment for the swan in the story. The sound goes straight to my heart. I look for Ljuba, who walks quickly on ahead of me, despite her size. I try to grab her hand, but she is wearing thick leather mittens. My hand slips away from hers. She didn't even notice that I'd tried to hold it.

'We planted flowers here,' she says like an expert. 'If you want, you can plant some, too.'

I say nothing. The grave takes work, she means, but she's been taking care of it for a long time now. Baba Sara and her husband, whom I never met, are in there. Ljuba talks about visiting her relatives with a self-evidence that is completely foreign to me. You have to come often; the grass will take over the slab, but if your cleaning powder is too strong, it kills all the grass. She tips out the satchel of cleaning equipment that she carries with her like a miniature doctor's bag. I'm holding a bouquet of flowers wrapped in bright tissue paper. It's cold and the flowers' red heads are already drooping.

On our way between the graves, we don't see anyone I can greet, just to break the silence that reigns inside me. Ljuba talks without stopping. I would like to offer something, but nothing occurs to me. Finally she turns to me and says, 'Here we are.'

A pale cloud of breath floats before her reddened face.

I stare at Ljuba's half-hidden mouth, as the cloud slowly fades. The grave is behind her.

I look at the spikes on the small wrought-iron fence that encloses it and reach into my coat pocket for my compact mirror.
Even with gloves on, I can feel its perfectly smooth sides.

'Some people say you couldn't care less.'

She stands in my way and waits.

'You didn't get in touch once.'

I look at her and don't answer.

'You're the only one who didn't get in touch, Mischka.'

I slowly pull the mirror out of my pocket and hold it in my
closed fist.

'I didn't want to tell you in front of all the others.'

I open my fingers and the mirror, holding it in my hand so that
I can look in the mirror but without holding it up between us. I
don't see any tears. She follows my eyes and slaps my hand hard.
Without warning. The impact burns on my fingertips. The mirror
sails in a high arc and breaks open on a stone.

Her chest is heaving. I can make out the little hairs on her fur
coat bending up and back down. I go round her. She doesn't move.
I can hear her breathing and quiet sobs. I can't feel my breath.

I put the flowers down on the edge of the grave the way you
put your hat on a rack in the entrance hall before going into the
living room. I take off my boots and sit.

'Mischka!'

The tombstone is old and its sides are crumbling. I can feel the
cold that the long winter has stored up in the stone on my rear
end and the soles of my feet despite my quilted skirt and thick,
hand-knit socks.

Red flowers next to red socks on grey stone.

'Mischka, I'm sorry.'

Two pictures are inlaid in the stone. Two semicircular pictures of my grandparents – one very old and weathered, with an unknown face, next to it, Baba Sara's friendly face – and right underneath, my father. He's laughing. He has a black beard. He's young. Above the picture is his name in gold letters. I study it for a long time and pay close attention to what I'm feeling inside.

I don't feel anything but the cold, and that ever more clearly.

I slip my boots back on and stand up.

Behind the stone lies my mirror. It didn't break. Only the lid popped open under the force of the blow.

'Let's go?' I ask.

Ljuba wipes the tears from her face with her coat sleeve. Her mascara has run. She sniffles loudly. She puts her hand on my shoulder, then both arms. She hugs me tight. Her brown fur coat covers my face. Her warmth closes around me like a diving bell. Her perfume is heavy.

'You silly goose,' she whispers in my ear.

I leave the mirror behind in the dry grass.

Ljuba doesn't pick it up, either.

'He's not here any more anyway,' I say.

We go back in silence through the fog, along the empty paths, back to the heavy fence that secures the graveyard.

I stop at the exit.

Before us is a busy street that immediately drenches us in big city noise. The cars have turned on their headlights and their beams roll over me. Everything is back in motion.

'Would you take me by our old apartment, Ljuba?'

She looks at me in surprise.

'If it's still there,' I add, and sit down in the middle of the street because my feet have suddenly given out. Everything is spinning.

Several passersby head our way, but before they can reach us, Ljuba has pulled me to my feet.

'Everything's fine. Everything's fine.' She smiles, and keeps an iron grip on my collar. She says quietly to me, 'I'll call a taxi.'

'Quiet,' Ljuba says, having followed my wish, reluctantly, but still, she followed. I lift my hand, but she overtakes me and pushes the doorbell into the plastic socket with her pink, padded thumb. I expect a shrill noise, or something that rings exactly like it did back then, a ring that will mean something to me, that could give me back something. There is no noise. Ljuba presses again, and we are once again surrounded by silence.

Ljuba knocks vigorously on the door. Inside, I hear shuffling steps. All of a sudden I want to turn and go, as Ljuba raps one more time and the door swings open.

I see a large, dark foyer that I recognize instantly and, at the back, the door to our two rooms and to Aunt Musja's little room.

A small woman with big hair stands in the doorway.

'For who?' She's curt.

I choke.

'Mrs Musja.'

She looks at me closely.

'I see. Did you call earlier?'

'Yes, yes, we…' Ljuba bustles, unpeeling herself from her big shawl as she pushes through the door to make room for me.

'She's waiting. Come in. I'll bring you to her.'

I catch her mistrustful look again. She turns and I recognize the way she moves, how she turns her head, the colour of the long strands of hair hanging down. I don't want to call her name; she doesn't seem to recognize me. My friend Lenka. She opens the door to our rooms. I almost want to believe we'll keep going straight, into my parents' room, and sit in front of the television by the fireplace, like always. But she turns right and opens the door to Aunt Musja's room with her prettily manicured hand. The door is narrow and we squeeze through. Does she remember how we destroyed this room?

Her room is still full of knickknacks, but I'm struck by how meagre and constricted it is. I had never noticed it as a child. The air is heavy with smoke and perfume and the smell of a very old lady. I stand stupidly on the threshold and say, 'Hello.'

She's sitting in her canopy bed, a small, dried-up body covered with thousands of frills: frills on her nightgown, on her blanket, on the pillows, a giant proliferation of dirty white and her hair still twisted in red curls. I have to think of Vivienne Westwood, like a bizarre publicity campaign. She's wearing lipstick, which shines out of her pale little face in a happy-loony smile.

Next to the bed is a commode and under this is a pair of colourful stiletto-heeled shoes. Lenka is still in the doorway.

'Grandma Musja?' she asks. 'Would you like a cup of tea? I've just put the kettle on.'

Without answering her, Musja offers me a small crystal bowl filled with little egg-shaped sweets. All three of us stand there without saying a word.

'Take one, honey,' Musja giggles.

Lenka grins and avoids my eye.

'Do you know who I am?' I ask warily.

'Take one! Take! Take!'

'Mrs Musja–' I begin importantly.

'Oh, take one! You always did before, without even asking,' she interrupts me. 'And so did that one!'

She points her thin finger at Lenka, who automatically takes a step back.

'Maybe you should step outside,' Lenka says softly. 'She's very worked up today. That's not good.'

'Take one!' Musja screeches.

I reach out and take one obediently. The sweets are stuck to each other and hard as rock.

'Now it's fine,' murmurs Musja, looking very satisfied, 'and now sit with me.'

I roll the two sweets from one hand to the other.

'Sit down!' she says shrilly.

I approach her bed but remain standing. The sour, powdery smell gets stronger.

'I wanted to bring you greetings,' I offer.

'Sit down,' she repeats, this time more softly, and I lower myself onto the edge of her bed.

'From Laura, my mother.'

'That's good,' she whispers, and in an instant is fast asleep. The crystal bowl slips from her fingers. I put it back on her night table, which is covered with little bottles.

Lenka sighs and shrugs helplessly.

The kettle is whistling so loudly in the distant kitchen that we can even hear it in here.

'May I just go and turn it off?' Ljuba calls in from the hall.

'I've been taking care of her for five years,' Lenka whispers. 'She has no-one. And then... later... I'll get her room. We set it up that way.'

She's still mistrustful.

'But, Lenka, come on, I'm not one of her relatives.' It slips out of me. 'And I don't need her room, either. I just wanted to see it all again, you know?'

Her eyes get big and round before they narrow again.

'Who are you?' she turns on me. 'Who are you and how do you know who lives here and what my name is?'

'Lenka,' I say, and I feel the tears that ran dry at the graveyard rise inside me. 'But, Lenka, we played here with Schenya. You must remember.'

'What's with the kettle?' Ljuba calls in, and Musja stirs uneasily on her pillows.

'My name is Elena,' Lenka snaps. 'And I haven't seen Evgeny for ten years. And I don't want to have anything to do with him, either. Now get out.'

I turn and go.

Our apartment door is in front of me, closed. I lift my hand and push the bronze handle. It gives. The door is unlocked and swings open.

Through the opening, I see our chimney, the marble slabs, the open hole in the wall and horrible carpeting everywhere. The parquet floor has been painted dark brown. There's a large table between the fireplace and the door, and behind it, the frightened face of an old lady laying out cards.

'Shut the door!' she shouts. 'This is the fourth time this week! You could at least knock, God damn it – Lenka, now really!'

'They're not with me,' she promptly trills, and slams the door in my face. My childhood disappears with a hollow thud.

'Get out! I don't want any trouble here like there was with Evgeny, understood?'

'Lenka – Elena, please, I just wanted to see you again,' I whisper. 'You're the only one I remember, you and Schenya; you're my only friends.'

'Is that so?' she snarls at me. 'Then why didn't you ever write back? Get lost!'

And with that, she shoves me towards the door, as a befuddled Ljuba comes towards us from the kitchen carrying a tray filled with tea, and sugar, and biscuits.

'What right did you have to do this?' Lenka starts in on her.

'The neighbour let me,' Ljuba defends herself.

'She doesn't have anything to do with this! Which neighbour, anyway? Out! Get out, both of you!'

'But those are my biscuits,' comes from the kitchen, 'and I'm inviting everyone who wants some.'

Ljuba sets the tray on the telephone table with dignity.

Our spy's seat is empty.

'I don't care to accept your hospitality in any case. Come, Mischka. Let's go.'

'Mischenka! Stay!' someone calls from the kitchen.

'Who on earth is that?' I'm stunned.

'No idea.' Ljuba is evidently easily upset. 'But she likes visitors.'

Cursing, Lenka grabs the tray. The cups clatter as she turns and disappears down the long corridor that leads to the kitchen.

I wipe my eyes. They're dry.

'Come, Mischka,' Ljuba insists. 'Come. She's afraid for her room. What do you think it's like, at twenty-five, to have to live with your parents in a single room? Don't hold it against her. Anyhow, we were here. Now, please, come.'

'What's with Schenya?' I whisper.

Ljuba looks away.

She takes my elbow. I pull away.

'What happened with him?'

'He's in prison. And no more questions.'

She turns decisively on her heel and opens the front door.

On the floor near my foot lies a sugar cube. I want to pick it up and put it in my pocket with the sweets, but I change my mind at the last moment when I catch a glimpse of myself, my distorted reflection mirrored in the black side of the telephone, and I crush the sugar cube with my winter boot.

I feel strangely apprehensive at the thought of trying to find out more about Schenya.

When the door closes behind us, I know I'll never come here again.

That evening, when, for a moment, I'm not being watched, I slip into my cousins' bedroom, past the plastic chest I secretly painted with them when I was five, just before we forced Adrian to eat dirty snow. I think of my daughter's face, which looks so much like mine. She's waiting for me in Vienna. I chase the thought away, push aside the plastic curtain and look for a long time out into the emptiness of the outskirts. A skyline of blinking red lights and factory smokestacks. I stood here like this last time, with a glass of children's champagne in my hand. I feel an imperceptible movement, a draught. I lift my hand to the pane of glass, to see if there is a crack in the weather stripping.

A strange face looks at me, mirrored in the window. Without a neck, nebulous, flatter and much bigger than my own, which I can see reflected within it. I recognize him right away. Splithead.

The vortex that rises and falls lazily within his gelatinous shell has the colours of the sky on a white night. He has no recognizable features. His interior is constantly shifting. It billows, pulsates around my head and washes over me. His eyes, dark, bottomless holes with no pupils or whites, stare at me. They're enormous. They make the terrifying face look childish. Cute.

I approach him carefully, until my nose and forehead touch the cool glass. I dive through him into the courtyards of St Petersburg. I no longer see anything but the surrounding houses.